W9-BPN-564

Tumbling through galactic space THE
GLAIVE bears this message:

From the sky will come the Black Fortress.
From the Fortress will come the Slayers to
devour the planet of Krull.
Then shall a girl of ancient name become
queen, and the king she chooses shall rule
the planet. And their son shall rule the
galaxy.

Imbued with a fearsome power THE
GLAIVE can be a wondrous weapon. In the
hands of the right man it can save the planet

KRULL

Also by Alan Dean Foster

THE THING

and published by Corgi Books

Alan Dean Foster

KRULL

Based upon a screenplay by
Stanford Sherman

CORGI BOOKS

KRULL

A CORGI BOOK 0 552 12278 5

First publication in Great Britain

PRINTING HISTORY
Corgi edition published 1983
Corgi edition reprinted 1983

Copyright © 1983 by Columbia Pictures Industries, Inc.
All rights reserved.

Conditions of sale
1: This book is sold subject to the condition that it
shall not, by way of trade *or otherwise*, be lent, re-sold,
hired out or otherwise *circulated* without the publisher's
prior consent in any form of binding or cover other than
that in which it is published *and without a similar
condition including this condition being imposed on
the subsequent purchaser.*

2: This book is sold subject to the Standard Conditions
of Sale of Net Books and may not be re-sold in the UK
below the net price fixed by the publishers for the book.

Corgi Books are published by Transworld Publishers Ltd.,
Century House, 61–63 Uxbridge Road,
Ealing, London W5 5SA.
Printed and bound in Great Britain by
Cox & Wyman Ltd., Reading, Berks.

For Kathleen Malley,
*For carrying the banner and
with thanks for the confidence ...*

KRULL

I

The boy pulled the collar of his coat tighter against his neck. It was a damp, chilly morning. The first suggestions of winter reached thin, icy fingers down from the North Country. Soon the land would sleep beneath a thick mantle of white wet down.

Nearby the flock cropped methodically at the long grass. They would work their way to the top of the gentle slope, perhaps as far as the large boulder protruding like a giant's nose from the hillside, before it was dark and time to herd them in. The boy thought hungrily of the steaming stewpot that awaited him back in the village, of the hot tea that could drive out a day's chill as it spread outward in a steadily warming circle from his belly.

Life was not easy, his father repeatedly told him, but with a little hard work it might be made bearable. The sheep would provide meat for the coming year, their wool would give warmth, and there should be enough of both left over to trade for money in the marketplace. They might even make enough money to travel to his cousin's hometown of Banbreak, where there was much talk of uniting all the towns and villages in the region to form a kingdom. The boy's father was all for such unification. A single government could provide strength and protection from which all might prosper. There was too much division and argument among men, especially now, when they ought to join together against a common enemy.

The dominant ram let out a nervous *baa* and the boy stirred himself. It wouldn't do to be caught daydreaming. Standing atop the little knoll he'd chosen for a resting place, he leaned on his staff and carefully inspected the surrounding terrain. You never could tell what might be lurking out there, crouched low among the bushes or in the rustling branches up a tree. He prided himself on his watchfulness. Since the flock had been entrusted to his care, he'd lost not a single sheep to marauders, no matter whether they approached on four legs or two or eight.

The ram let out a second bleat and there were echoes from others in the flock. They began to mill together uncertainly, clustering around the mature rams and ignoring the grass. The boy's fingers tightened on the staff as he turned a slow circle, trying to pinpoint the source of their unease. He could see nothing. In the trees all that moved were wind-stirred leaves, on the ground nothing but rippling grass and weeds. As if to worry him further a stiff breeze suddenly sprang to life, bending the taller bushes and rattling the gravel underfoot.

Then it occurred to the boy that it had become preternaturally silent. There were no bird sounds, no digger barks, not even the buzz of omnipresent insects from the small stream that flowed nearby.

The wind intensified, swirling his cloak around him. It was rapidly growing darker. Storm coming up, he thought. Probably from behind Ignatus Mountain. But that wasn't sufficient to explain the flock's eerie behavior. They were all bleating now, crying out anxiously. Still the source of their collective distress remained hidden from sight.

No matter. He did not have any more time to hunt for invisible threats. His job now was to get the flock under cover before the storm broke. Still keeping a wary eye on the nearest clump of cover, which might conceal a lurking predator, he hopped down from his perch and began shooing the sheep back toward the village.

They refused to budge, clustering so tightly together they threatened to trample the lambs. Now what the devil had got into those fool animals?

He turned his gaze upward, the better to gauge the speed and strength of the approaching storm, and his jaw dropped.

The lowing sky was full of dark cumulus, but the largest cloud of all was not drifting southward with its billowy companions. It was falling steadily earthward. Lights flickered along its gray black sides and a dull hum came from somewhere within. The wind rose to a shriek as displaced air sought escape.

The young shepherd stared, as paralyzed as his sheep. Now he understood the source of their frozen panic, knew why they clustered helplessly together instead of trying to run to safety. The cloud that wasn't a cloud covered most of the little valley and there was nowhere to run to.

Trees snapped and popped like dead twigs as the Fortress of the Beast settled gently to the ground, obliterating anything less resistant than granite beneath its great weight. Only one had observed its unannounced arrival. Gradually the birds resumed their forays from those trees that had been spared. Insects reemerged from their hiding places to restake their claim to the world.

Of the shepherd and his flock there was only a memory.

*　　*　　*

One by one the sun made silhouettes of the horsemen as they topped the narrow ridge. It was just after daybreak, but the horses heaved and their riders' legs ached as they clutched at their mounts' flanks. Horses and men had been on the road since well before sunup.

Now they started down the steep grade, scrambling toward the next ridge. There were five, lightly laden. On the long ride heavy armor would have been a hindrance.

The last of them seemed unsure of his seat, swaying forward and back as though drunk. The swaying increased until the man's eyes closed and he tumbled from the saddle. As he rolled over and over down the slope, he left a trail behind him, crimson spotting the rocks and brush with the passing of his life.

One of the riders slowed, working hard to keep his mount from stumbling. The lead rider, who'd been picking his way down the hillside with reckless skill, also reined in and turned to look back to where their companion had come to rest against an outjutting rock.

"No, Masreck!" the leader shouted. "There's no time, and he's finished."

"But, Lord Colwyn, Eric's my cousin!"

"He was your cousin. Leave him where he's come to final rest or we're all done for. Too many lost already to risk everything for one who can no longer help. Does he move?"

The soldier carrying the banner spoke through clenched teeth as he stared dully at the motionless body. "No, m'lord. He lies still."

"Then save your regrets for later and pray for his soul as we ride. We all have regrets to pay for this journey." He turned away and spurred his horse on, down the steep grade, over the gully splitting the bottom, then up the opposite slope and into the dense forest beyond. Nearby rode an old man wearing the crown of a king, his regal garb now thick with road dirt and dried mud.

The men were tired but Colwyn dared not risk halting for a rest or a meal. The land was full of the strange creatures men had come to call Slayers. Time enough to rest when the evil had been purged from the land.

Soon they splashed into the River Eiritch, men and horses alike glad of the cold spray many hooves kicked upward. Another month would see the river transformed into an impossible torrent by Endsummer rains. But today it was fordable. Grime and filth was vanquished by the cleansing spray and when they emerged on the far side, the light of Krull's twin suns quickly commenced to dry the refreshed riders.

Before long they broke from the forest, climbing onto the High Plains. Snowcapped peaks rose still higher in the distance.

Against the backdrop of gray stone and blue sky their destination stood stark and beautiful, a cloud come to rest on the hard earth.

Colwyn stood in his stirrups and pointed. "There! The White Castle of Eirig."

"We're not there yet, m'lord," the warrior holding the standard reminded him.

"By the Shadows, we're near enough!" Colwyn looked back over his shoulder. "No sign of Slayers. They have everything a good fighter should have save initiative, for which we can be thankful."

"We're likely to find out soon enough, sir," said another of the soldiers.

"Aye," agreed a third.

Colwyn favored the old man breathing hard in the saddle alongside with a look of concern. "Father? We could rest a moment here."

"Not on my account," King Turold snapped. He wiped

river water from his beard. "Slip easy from the saddle after a ride like ours, my son, and you'll find it doubly hard to get going again. As you say, ahead waits the White Castle. Never did I think to see the day when I'd be glad of the sight."

"Desperate times, Father, force desperate accommodations."

"Aye, so you've tried to tell me these past months. Well, we've argued over it long and often, and this is no place for further debate." He urged his mount forward. Colwyn concealed a smile as he followed.

The White Castle was not as old as some. Its walls showed little damage from war and weather, the huge limestone blocks shining in the early morning light. Towers and battlements soared cloudward, challenging the sky. It combined in its construction all the best that the masons and architects of Krull could offer, providing a safe refuge in times of trouble and a vision of pale magnificence in times of peace. Columns were fluted like cave flowstone while grand archways provided entry to vast halls and a spacious, well-appointed courtyard. Those who had raised it were proud of their handiwork, and justly so, for it put all the other castles and fortresses of Krull to shame.

The woman who approached the parapet and placed delicate hands atop the white wall seemed to step from the imagination of some supremely skilled sculptor. A floating cloud of wispy bright hair framed her face, adding to her ethereal beauty as she turned to inspect the wide plains below the wall. Though her features were slight and her body slim, her resolve was manifest in both her expression and the way she carried herself before commoners as well as kings. Even to casual visitors it was clear there was something unique about Lyssa of Eirig.

Her father sensed it once again as he strode toward her. He tried to isolate that quality that defined Lyssa's difference but, as always, it continued to escape him. It was frustrating being unable to understand one's own offspring, but that did not keep him from admiring her or loving her.

He put a comforting hand around her waist and she smiled back at him for an instant before returning her gaze to the uninformative horizon.

"Colwyn and his escort should have been here a week ago, Father."

"The passes are patrolled by the Slayers. They like to fall upon incautious travelers. He may not have enough troops to break through."

"That would please you," she said dryly.

Eirig looked away from her. It was impossible to conceal one's true feelings from Lyssa. More than the slyest diplomat at court, she had a way of knowing when falsehoods spilled from a facile mouth. What an unreasonable and awkward talent for a daughter to possess!

"I sent men to help. Did I not send men to help? They were not requested, nor was I bound to send them. I did so only at your urging."

"Twenty men?" The rebuke was no less effective for the gentleness with which it was delivered.

"Our walls are thinly held. Most of the men are off to the east bringing in the harvest. Would you have me leave the castle defenseless, your own kinfolk and subjects, to aid a stranger who might well be beyond help? Have you now become a student of military matters as well as philosophy? Perhaps I should make you a field general in my army." This tirade he ventured without looking into her eyes.

"I sent what I could spare. These Slayers are everywhere. My first obligation is to protect Eirig. I could not send more."

"Our walls are paper so long as the Slayers roam our world with impunity," she replied. "I have read much history. Division and suspicion between kingdoms poison all of Krull.

They aid these Slayers as much as anything does. They are unlike any enemy we have fought. For once we must put ancient jealousies aside. We must have this alliance. You know that all the wise men are in favor of it.''

"Old fools," Eirig whispered. The knowledge that she was right did nothing to soften his heart. "Alliance with Turold, our ancient enemy! Marriage to his son. Nor is there any guarantee this alliance is what we need to defeat these Slayers.''

"No wise man gives guarantees, Father," she said consolingly. "That is one sign of wisdom.''

He turned away from her. "You spend too much time in books.''

"Every day we hear of another village burned by the Slayers," she said. "We must do something. This alliance can only strengthen us. I know it. All the signs say so.''

"You and your damned signs," he muttered. Strange woman, he mused. Daughter and stranger all at once.

"Father," she said calmly, "the past is a luxury, and past hatreds the most expendable luxury of all. Now we have only one enemy we must concern ourselves with: these Slayers who are enemy to us all. We must stop them somehow or they will make slaves of us all. I make this alliance with Turold's son for all Krull, for all the people. The common folk must know that against these invaders, the kingdoms stand united.''

Eirig leaned on the cool stone, his fingers working against each other. "If only it were anyone but Turold's son!''

"It must be Turold's son." There was no uncertainty in her voice. "It is right. You know that this is so.''

"Yes, yes, I know," Eirig rumbled. He'd given his approval to this match with the utmost reluctance.

"It will work, Father. It *has* to work, for all our sakes. I do not know what to expect from this marriage, but I will do what I must to make it work.''

Seeing that her musings were having little effect on him, she added, ''Colwyn is said to be a great fighter.''

''I worry for my daughter as well as for my people and for Krull,'' Eirig responded, a little less testily. ''I am allowed that much, surely.''

She smiled, put a hand on his arm. ''Of course you are, Father, and I love you for that.''

''Good fighters make bad husbands.''

''I respect your opinion, Father.'' She moved to kiss him before he could move out of the way. ''But there is no need for you to worry for me on that account. I am quite capable of taking care of myself.''

''I hardly need to be reminded of that,'' he fondly muttered.

''Perhaps you are right. If so, then it will be I who owes you the apologies.''

''I do not want your apologies,'' he said. ''I want your happiness.''

''There is but one way to know for certain if that is to be obtained.'' She returned to scouring the plain beneath the castle walls, her eyes traveling as far as the marshland that bordered the river.

''Perhaps,'' he admitted reluctantly. ''In any case, there's no need to exhaust yourself with these daily vigils. Go and rest; I will call you if by chance they should arrive this day.''

''Now, that is the common sense King Eirig is famed for.'' She left him with a smile as she strode from the wall.

Eirig followed her with his eyes. Strange girl. No, strange woman, he reminded himself. Her mother would have been proud of her. She was cast from the same unswerving mold.

In spite of all the good reasons she'd advanced, in his heart he still opposed this arranged marriage. But his mind concurred. His advisers were divided on the benefits the match might bring, being their usual quarrelsome selves, more a hindrance to his decision-making than a help. He'd been left to his own judgment. Heart say yea, mind say nay, and the two had warred within him many times these past difficult months.

Eventually his mind had barely won out, though even at this late date there were moments when he thought of calling the whole business off. He never reached that point. There was too much sense in his daughter's words. With them clung the nagging suspicion that she might be just the slightest bit smarter than her father.

The walls probed skyward above the exhausted horsemen as they urged their mounts over the last hundred yards. It was difficult to tell whether rider or beast was the more fatigued. Certainly both were in need of a long rest.

Colwyn leaned back in his saddle and shouted as they approached the parapet. "Mark the gate! Let us in!"

"Let who in?" an argumentative voice from above demanded to know. Another quickly shouted it down.

"By the serpents of the river, 'tis Prince Colwyn! And King Turold himself with him. Let them in!"

The massive gate swung inward. Colwyn led his companions forward into the courtyard. Light came from wall-mounted torches, adding to the haggard look presented by the riders. They were mobbed by a cluster of anxious attendants and men-at-arms.

"All the way from Turold . . . How did you slip through the Slayers? Did you come all that way, only the four of you . . . ?" The questions came too fast for ready reply, even had the riders been inclined to answer them.

The soldiers moved aside as their own lord approached with his royal escort. They would have to sit on their curiosity for a while longer.

Turold dismounted, concealing from the party of newcomers the ache in his numbed legs. Exhausted he might be, but he would not ask for assistance from his son's future father-in-law. Colwyn remained on his horse, mindful of procedure, though he thought it foolish.

The two kings regarded each other without affection. Turold was in no mood to bandy protocol. "We sent to you for help. More than one messenger departed and did not return with that aid. Though we have arrived in good health, it is through no thanks to you."

Eirig did not back down, though his daughter's accusation stuck in the back of his mind. "Your messengers never reached us. The Slayers spread a tight net, especially at night. Even so, twenty men were dispatched in hopes they might find you."

"We lost three hundred reaching here!" Turold replied angrily. "One hopeless rearguard action followed upon another so that we might make the 'safety' of these walls. The land between here and Turold is marked by too many graves. And you sent twenty men to help us."

"The Slayers are everywhere and this time of year the army of Eirig is more fiction than reality! Most of my fighting men are away bringing in the year's harvest, so that if the Slayers attack they cannot starve us out. I have my own people within these walls to worry about. Women and children. I did what I could." He took a belligerent step forward. "I did not choose this marriage, Turold."

"Nor did I, Eirig."

Colwyn had had about enough. Royal precedent be damned! He slid off his horse, stepped between them.

"I chose it," he said quietly.

Colwyn was not a big man. He had cousins who stood taller, marshaled more raw strength. But none were as quick. He had a tendency to brood, especially in the presence of persistent stupidity. There were those at the Turoldian court who thought him reckless and a bit too wild to wear the crown.

But none questioned his honesty or courage, and though no scholar, he had a way of penetrating obfuscation that allowed him to go straight to the heart of a problem, a talent most disconcerting to those schooled in the arts of argument and debate. Unlike his relatives, he attracted no crowd of fawning sycophants. Put a query to Colwyn, it was said in Turold, and you will have a straight answer right off, but for your sake it had best be a worthwhile question.

"Your daughter chose it," he went on, speaking to Eirig. He looked back to his own father, then again at the king who had welcomed them with something less than open arms. "It will be done. Argue all you wish, fight if it pleases you, but nothing will prevent this marriage. This alliance must be made.

"Now if you will excuse me, I would like to greet my bride." He turned from them both and inspected the court-yard. After a moment's study he started for the doorway leading into the keep, walking as though the way were well known to him.

Eirig could not find words to stop him, but neither was he willing to let a mere boy depart their confrontation having the last word. He gestured back at Turold and the two surviving members of the escort.

"And is this the great army you will join with Eirig to lead against the Slayers?"

Colwyn paused partway up the stairs. His voice was firm, assured as he replied. "Whatever army I have I will lead against them. I brought two warriors with me. If Eirig can provide two as good, then I will have an army of five.

"This I do know. I will not squat cowering behind castle walls, neither here nor in Turold, and wait for the Slayers to

come for me the way a pig waits for its butcher. The Slayers
are used to being the attackers. Perhaps it will surprise them
to be the defenders for a change, no matter what size the
force that goes against them. I will fight them, King Eirig,
with whatever army I can raise from your land and mine and
whichever other might choose to join me.'' He resumed his
climb, hesitating again at the top of the staircase.

"I will fight them until I have won, or am dead.'' He
disappeared into the castle.

Eirig stared after him, then turned back to his royal
counterpart. "I do not know if he has your skill at arms,
Turold, but the boy surely has inherited your tongue.''

Turold looked past his host, toward the portal that had
swallowed up his son. "There is more to the youth than that,
Eirig. Sometimes I do not understand him. Sometimes I think
he sees with other than his eyes. Even the wise men of my
court are in awe of him and not a few are afraid. A most
unusual son. On balance I know he is more blessing than
curse, but there are moments that give me pause. In truth,
there are.''

Eirig digested that, then frowned. It seemed to him that this
was not the first time such thoughts had been expressed with
respect to a royal offspring.

I hate these damned great castles, Colwyn thought as he
made his way into the central hall. He slowed and thought to
wipe some of the sweat and grime from his face. Around him
brightly colored banners and insignia of territory hung limp
from the rafters. Torches flickered on mounted armor. Eirig's
kingdom was not particularly rich but it was extensive. Its
people were not given to ostentatious displays of wealth. In
that respect they had much in common with Turold.

It was not money that he sought from the alliance, but
brave men ready to fight for their homes and their world. The

wise men at court had tried to show him that such an
adventure was doomed from the start. The depredations of the
Slayers could not be prevented; even to think of doing so was
foolishness. It was best to accept one's fate, much as one did
a harsh winter or summer flood.

Colwyn refused to accept the inevitability of disaster that
some of the wise men had forecast. There was no fear in him
of the Black Fortress, nor of the shadowy master it was home
to. It did not terrify him that the Fortress apparently came
from another world. Just because this affliction was new and
alien did not mean it couldn't be cured.

Slayers could be slain like any man, for all that they
possessed horrible weapons and did not fight like men. All
that was required was the will to fight them, the will and an
army of dedicated warriors. Between them, Eirig and Turold
might mount such an army.

He started forward again, stumbled over his own tired feet,
and caught himself. His gaze darted leftward. There had been
the briefest giggle.

His eyes stopped at a half-opened doorway. Even in the
dimly lit hall it would have been difficult to pass over that
flash of color.

Lyssa did not laugh again. She stepped out into the light.
Her dress was finely but not elaborately embroidered and she
was as clean as Colwyn was sweaty. Their eyes met and all
such simple thoughts were instantly put aside.

She's so slight, Colwyn mused. A strong breath could blow
her away. Or could it? There was something about her that
suggested otherwise. A thin tree can have strong roots, he
reminded himself. Slim but strong, then, in mind as well as
body. Such was the Lyssa he'd been led to expect. She came
toward him.

"I have chosen well," she said softly, without guile.

It was there, he thought. The power he sensed deep within

her, the same power that had been in her letters. It was in her voice too, every syllable, for all that they were softly uttered. He had thought to greet a much larger woman, but as he continued to stare at her she expanded in his eyes.

"So have I," he thought to murmur.

"Handsome." Her inspection was direct. "I had not counted on that. It would not have made a difference, but I suppose it's good that a wife should find her husband pleasant to look upon."

"Life is long and full of mornings," he responded. "One should not be displeased by the first face one sees every day."

"You speak of days to come. I see by your appearance that the past ones were not as promising. Your journey was as difficult as it was delayed?"

"But necessary. The land between Eirig and Turold is filled with the misery inflicted by the Slayers. We left as many as we could lying in the fields they had destroyed."

"You boast of killing?"

"I never boast of killing. There is nothing praiseworthy in making murder."

She nodded slowly. "I was told that you were brave but until now did not know what my advisers meant when they kept telling me you were not the usual sort of warrior. You are wise. And handsome as well. A rare combination." She spread out the folds of her dress and did a little pirouette for him. "Then, you do find me attractive?"

"These past months I've had to deal with innumerable idiotic questions at court. Do not ask me more of the same." He grinned slightly.

"I think I like you, master of the indirect compliment." More seriously she inquired, "How fares your homeland against the Slayers?"

"No worse than most and better than many. They seem to

be attacking the poorer kingdoms and smaller towns first. Our turn will surely come if they are not stopped."

"You believe they can be stopped?"

"They can be killed, though they do not die like men. I do not side with those who believe it is our fate to be overrun by them. I do not believe in inevitable happenings. If I did I would not have made this marriage against my father's wishes."

"Nor I against mine."

"We shouldn't waste time. Will the ceremony be held here?" He indicated the vastness of the great hall.

"No, there is a special place within the castle. Tonight, at moonrise, we will begin according to the ancient rites. I have no love for ritual but my father has insisted. He desires that you prove yourself."

"I don't doubt it." He went quiet, his thoughts momentarily elsewhere.

Say something, Lyssa told herself as the silence deepened between them. The man is uncomfortable. Help him to relax. You are to be husband and wife, not business partners.

"My father says that good fighters make bad husbands."

"I too have heard that, only the other way round. What does your mother say?"

"My mother died when I was small. I scarcely remember her. No"—she put a hand to his lips to restrain him from mouthing the usual condolences. "It is long done with and now is not the time to look to the past." She smiled reassuringly at him. "Some say it depends on the husband. What would you say?"

A woman as clever as she was beautiful, Colwyn mused. All that he had been told seemed truth. There were many attractive damsels in both kingdoms, many princesses in kingdoms close by, but only one Lyssa of Eirig.

"I would say that peace and love, whether established

between nations or man and woman, depend not on believing old tales and superstitions but rather on forging a relationship free of the meanderings of others.''

Her smiled widened. "A good answer . . . Colwyn. I believe this match is well met.'' She leaned forward and kissed him lightly. The brief touch reminded him of the hot breath from a kitchen oven quickly opened and as quickly shut again. It was both welcoming and promising. They separated with reluctance.

"Proprieties,'' she whispered, glancing past him to make certain the great hall was still empty and that no one had observed. "We will marry only once, so we must take care to do it properly. I am sure of you, but we must be certain of each other.'' Her hand brushed his cheek lightly. Then she turned and retreated back through the door from which she'd emerged.

Colwyn stared until the door had closed behind her. His cheek burned where she'd touched him. He was aware that his hands were still steepled together as if still holding hers, and that he was holding his breath like a swimmer who'd just crossed a goodly distance underwater. He exhaled slowly.

The Slayers had best beware. With such a woman at his side he felt there was nothing he couldn't do.

II

No one could remember who had designed the nexus. The architect of the castle was little more than an honored memory and the plans he had drawn were buried somewhere in the royal archives. The nexus was a special place, utilized only for the most profound ceremonies.

Nor was the reason for its design immediately apparent to the casual observer. An advanced mathematician would have noted the schematic with a start of surprise, but there were no advanced mathematicians in Eirig now.

Two corridors wound a strange course through the lower part of the white castle, twisting and turning until they finally met at the nexus. A small altar and water basin that filled from a stone spigot dominated the far end of the chamber.

Distant music penetrated the special place, but few of those participating in the ceremony paid it much attention. Eirig and Lyssa approached down one corridor while from the end of the other Colwyn and his father anxiously awaited the bride's arrival. Colwyn was impatient for the proceedings to be over and done with, but he did not try to hurry matters. He remembered what Lyssa had said about observing the proprieties.

The men-at-arms kept their eyes forward as the royal pair walked between their ranks, though several could not keep themselves from stealing a look at the exquisitely beautiful Lyssa as she passed them by. Everyone knew that she had turned down many suitors and each man privately measured himself against this successful visitor, the solemn-faced Colwyn of Turold. There was little envy in their thoughts, however. Most of all there was admiration mixed with hope. All knew what benefits the alliance with their powerful neighbor to the west could bring.

As Lyssa's torch passed each opposing pair of soldiers, their own torches sprang to life. Though they had been warned, the sudden combustion still came as a shock. It was this power of the princess's that had put off more than one weak-spined suitor, the power that danced in her eyes and could make the strongest man go queasy in the belly. That such an implied threat had not dissuaded this Colwyn was the strongest point in his favor.

And as Colwyn's own torch had given light to the torches held by the men in the other corridor, glances of approval had come from the men-at-arms. Here at last was a fit match for their princess. Who could predict what good might come of such a union?

They met at last in the domed chamber that was the nexus, the ancient place of bringing-together, the sanctuary where those of power might demonstrate secret truths to one another.

As was his right, Turold spoke first, his voice firm and unwavering. "From this day, my kingdom is no more."

Colwyn removed his hand from the torch he held together with his father. His eyes were half-closed and it almost looked as if he might be falling asleep. But he was more than alert. The torch went out. He blinked and turned to face his bride.

"Nor is mine," Eirig said, assured at last that this Turoldian might be a fit match for his daughter.

Lyssa let go of their firebrand and the flame fled from the wood as quickly as it had from its counterpart. Turold took a step forward, extended a hand, and placed it on King Eirig's upper arm. Eirig reciprocated.

"A single kingdom under our children. From this day forward let no man speak for Turold or for Eirig. Let our people mingle free and unafraid with each other and help one another in times of prosperity as well as chaos. If any more blood is to be spilt in either land, let it be not the blood of brothers but of Slayers!"

"Agreed," said Eirig quietly. The import of this moment had wiped out most of his lingering doubts, and there was gruff friendship in Turold's tone. "Now to the great hall, that the marriage ceremony may be properly concluded and the bond fastened."

Both pairs turned and started up the right-hand corridor. Colwyn and Lyssa marched side by side behind their fathers, careful to keep their eyes from each other. The ponderousness of ceremony weighed heavily on Colwyn and he was anxious to be done with speeches and invocations. Lyssa's sideways glances counseled patience and she whispered without turning her head: "Gentle go, husband-to-be. All this will be over and done with soon enough."

"I have no taste for these primitive rituals," he muttered back at her.

"They are necessary. The books say it is so."

"The books have been of little help to us in combating the Slayers. Why should I take their advice where marriage is concerned?"

"Because I ask it of you, Colwyn."

He couldn't repress a grin. "Do I detect the sound of hands clapping?"

She fell a step off his pace. "Only if you cannot see that I follow you around."

Eirig looked back at them. They were starting up a circular staircase. "Quiet, the both of you! Remember your positions."

"I will strive to do so, Father, when the proper time comes."

He made a face at her but said nothing. Perhaps it would not be such a hard thing, to give away so impertinent a child.

The wedding party emerged from the stairwell and entered the great hall. At the far end, to one side of the throne, was a font filled with freshly drawn springwater. The music which had filled the castle all evening was drowned out by the sound of swords beating on shields as the king's guard acknowledged the approach of the bridal couple.

Lyssa and Colwyn halted before the stone basin, their fathers looking on approvingly. A single torch stood upright in a metal sconce nearby. Colwyn stepped forward and removed it from its resting place. It burst into flame without so much as a glance. Murmurs of approval rose from the watching ranks of soldiers. Here was a man they could follow. Yet the critical test was still to come.

Colwyn composed himself. Again it seemed as if he were half-asleep as he spoke. No one could tell for certain if he was addressing them all, his bride-to-be only, or the wood he held tightly in his right hand.

"I give fire to water. It will not return to me except from the hand of the woman I choose as my wife." Eirig in particular was watching closely as Colwyn recited. Were the old books right? Was this the match they sometimes alluded to?

Colwyn held the flaming brand over the basin and let it fall. It dropped like a fisherman's line and landed upright on the bottom. Beneath the surface it continued to burn as brightly as ever. A great sigh arose from the onlookers while King Turold looked proud.

The sentry who stood atop the gate cursed his rotten luck at pulling guard duty on this night of all nights. Here he was, stuck out in the damp and cold, while most of his brethern were inside the keep, their armor polished and sparkling, enjoying the wedding ceremony.

Something broke his train of thought. He stopped and stared out into the night: black as a lawyer's thoughts. But surely he'd heard something moving about.

There it was again. Rain, he decided. A late summer squall moving toward the castle. He would get drenched. His more fortunate colleagues would tease him about his bad luck later that night back in the barracks.

He strained to hear better: a mighty strong storm. He turned and called out. Several other sentries came running from their stations to join him in staring out into the darkness. They listened intently.

"That's not rain, I think," said one. "Surely those are hoofbeats?"

"Nay," another argued, " 'tis only rain, or the wind blowing out from the forest."

They bent toward the rising rush, trying to reach out into the blackness, wanting to be certain before committing themselves. There was a royal wedding in progress and no man wanted to raise the alarm falsely.

Lyssa stepped toward the font and studied the fire burning steadily beneath the water. She did not close her eyes, nor did she look the least bit sleepy. Her movements and words were crisp, businesslike. But she could not hide the slight trembling that afflicted her. She was shaking from the effort required to prepare. Nothing must go wrong. She'd waited too long for this moment.

"I take fire from water. I give it only to the man whom I choose as my husband."

Fingers spread, she reached out and down, one tiny hand hovering an inch above the water. For a long moment nothing happened. The torch continued its miraculous burn. Eirig held his breath.

There was the faintest hiss, loud in the respectful silence, as she reached into the water and removed her hand. She turned it palm-up and opened her fingers, showing flames dancing hotly on pale skin. The air of expectancy in the hall was almost palpable.

She turned to extend her fiery palm to Colwyn. Her voice dropped to a whisper and her face glowed as her entire being seemed suffused with the heat from the fire that flickered in her hand.

"Colwyn. Now is the time. Before my father and my people, before all of Krull. Before the words that fill the old books. I ask thee most sweetly. Take the fire from my hand."

"Rain, you think?" The sentry was tired. "It sure sounds like rain coming. You're all of you crazy if you think otherwise. I'm getting back to my post before the watch commander finds me out of position." He hesitated, listened hard as he stared into the darkness. The thunder was growing steadily louder, and there was an unnatural steadiness to it.

Then, as his stunned companions looked on, the skeptic toppled slowly backward off the wall. Something bright and deadly had struck him in the chest.

The others scattered, frantically trying to sound the alarm. Their shouts were unnecessary and unheard, as the sound of the explosion that blew apart the main gate aroused everyone in the castle courtyard. Fragments of wood and stone flew in all directions while thin shards of light and bursts of energy felled one soldier after another.

The noise reached to the hall and broke the hopeful mood that had enveloped the ceremony. Colwyn wavered slightly and Lyssa's eyes broke from his.

"Slayers! Inside the gate!" the words rang out. Wedding ceremony forgotten, soldiers turned and rushed for the courtyard.

"Arm yourselves!" Turold roared to the gathering.

"But the ceremony!" Lyssa pleaded.

"No time for that now." Colwyn turned away from her, impatient to join the fight.

The moment had cracked. Time later to mend it. Lyssa's hand became a fist. When she opened her hand again, the flame that had burned there so intensely had vanished. She hurried after Colwyn, cursing the formal gown that hampered her movements.

"We'll fight them together," she shouted.

"No, not here."

"But the ceremony—"

"Can be completed later. For the moment my concern is for your safety, not our future."

"Colwyn, think a moment. Our safety lies in our future."

"Soon," he told her soothingly. "The mood is important." He turned, caught the attention of a captain of the King's Guard. "Get her to a place of safety."

"My place is with my men, fighting," the captain replied.

"Your place is where I order you to be." The captain hesitated a moment. But he'd heard the two kings join their kingdoms. He nodded tersely. "Get her away from this. We'll clear them out and there'll be plenty left for you."

"My place is with you," Lyssa insisted. "I'll not be shipped about at anyone's whim, not even yours."

Colwyn tried to divide his attention between his betrothed and the increasingly violent sounds beyond the hall.

"Do you love me?"

"I am to be your wife. The alliance—"

"Darkness and the Long Night take the alliance!" he snarled. *"Do you love me?"*

"The declaration of unity, I . . . yes. Yes, I love you, Colwyn."

He nodded once, then smiled gently. "Then do this for me. Go with the captain. Lead him if you cannot follow, but go."

She shook her head resignedly. "No time for wisdom, too much time for panic. I will do as you ask, but it is unfair of you to use so strong a lever."

"I don't care if you think it unfair of me. I care only that you are safe." He looked over at the captain. "Is there a safe way out of this castle?"

"An underground tunnel." Colwyn whirled, to find that it was Eirig, standing close by, who had spoken. "Little used recently. It would be the best way." Eirig spoke to the captain: "Lord Colwyn's orders are to be followed as though they were my own. Conduct the princess to Timrick City. We will send word when the castle has been secured. Take a suitable escort."

"Yes, sire." The captain turned away and began pulling soldiers from the ranks trying to push their way outside.

Eirig embraced his daughter. "We've had our disagreements, you and I. I cannot count the occasions when you made me angry enough to burst. Yet I think you have chosen your man well."

Colwyn tried to hide from the compliment. Compliments made him nervous.

"Take care, daughter."

"I will, Father."

"Enough," Colwyn yelled. The sounds of fighting were coming closer. "Get her out of here!"

Eirig nodded sharply to the captain, who saluted smartly and extended a hand to the princess. Lyssa accepted it, looking back over her shoulder as she departed.

"Come back to me, Colwyn!"

"It's not possible to conceive of anything else," he assured her. A hand came down on his shoulder. He found himself staring into the face of his father-in-law.

"Now then, my boy, there's killing to be done. The Slayers are many more than I thought. Never fear for your lady. She will get out safely." He cleared his throat self-consciously. "I won't try to hide the fact that I expressed more than one reservation about this match. There were many who agreed with me and argued about it. They sought to discredit you in my eyes. I see now that they were wrong. As always, Lyssa's judgment is proven sound. Come and fight alongside me."

"I'll be honored," said Colwyn. Together they moved toward the courtyard and the battle raging outside.

One of the guards cursed as he banged his head against a low beam. It was hard to see very far ahead, and the men were nervous.

"Captain," one man complained, "is there much more of this?"

"It leads beneath the walls and emerges far out in the hills. Hold your patience that long." He looked to his charge. "Is my lady all right?"

"I'm fine, Captain," Lyssa assured him, "but I don't like this place. I share your men's unease. Maybe it would be better to retrace our path and find a less confining egress. I know of a back window above the great hall. We could throw down a rope and escape by that route. Surely the Slayers will not be watching so precipitous an exit."

"Risky. Though I think the idea has merit, the king himself instructed me to go this way, and I have to follow his orders."

"I understand, Captain." Her eyes searched the corridor ahead, as if she could see farther than her escort. "Still, I am uncomfortable here."

"Rest assured we will soon be out in the—"

The Slayers who dropped from above cut the captain off in mid-sentence. Others dropped from rafters and beams behind, cutting off any retreat. In the narrow tunnel the sudden blasts of energy from the Slayers' strange spears mixed with the screams of dying men to overpower the senses. Those Slayers who fell perished with a single piercing, inhuman wail.

Lyssa picked up a knife and pressed her back against the corridor wall. Her retreat was cut off, as was the way out.

As she watched, one of the Slayers disengaged himself from the battle and moved toward her. She sliced at him with the knife, feinting as best she could before stabbing upward. She wasn't quite quick enough.

The knife barely pricked the Slayer as he twisted to the side. A powerful hand reached out to grasp her wrist. She tried to break free, trying not to stare into the empty holes in the creature's head where a face should be.

Several more of the massive figures moved to help the first. The knife was wrenched from her fingers. She felt herself rising in bloodless arms as she probed for her captor's eyes.

He did not have any.

Odd how they died, Colwyn thought as he swung the heavy sword in wide, sweeping arcs. It didn't matter how you slew them; a throat-thrust, a stab to the chest, a blow to the skull; all perished with the same unearthly scream before collapsing and disintegrating, save for the strange length of flesh that emerged to vanish by itself into the ground. Even when they dodged and stabbed, they seemed more dead than alive. They used no shouts, offered up no cries of mutual support as men did. Yet they fought together, communicating in some voiceless, cryptic fashion only another Slayer could comprehend.

And always there were more of them to cut down, as if the pattern from which they'd been stamped could repeat itself endlessly. The soldiers fought hard and well, but there are limits to what bravery and courage can accomplish. When a soldier fell, there was none to replace him. When a Slayer dropped, it seemed two more appeared to take his place.

Why now, he wondered? Why tonight this unprecedented assault on the White Castle? It seemed the fates intended the cruelest of jokes, to turn what should have been his happiest of days into one of darkness.

Or was there more to this attack than met the eye? What was the purpose behind it, if not simply more destruction? Certainly it seemed that the Slayers fought with an unaccustomed tenacity.

A glimpse of pale skin and dress near the ruined gate caught his attention. For the first time since the battle had been joined, his fury gave way to fear.

"Lyssa!"

She heard him call out and looked up toward his voice. Her hands were free to reach helplessly out to him. She rode the shoulder of a huge Slayer. There was no hint of blood, and her struggles told him that she had not been harmed. That was encouraging, and yet it was not. He did not care to think of what the Slayers wanted with a live captive. As she shouted his name, he forced himself to concentrate on killing.

He threw himself forward and began cutting a path toward her. The first Slayer to oppose him lost his head in a single stroke. Others hurried to intercept him. The whole direction of battle shifted subtly, as if the objective now were not the taking of the White Castle but the separation of the two lovers.

Though half-blinded by sweat, he did not pause to clear his eyes. He kept moving forward, the sword heavy in his hands. Off to one side he suddenly saw his father hard pressed to hold off several Slayers. At the same time he saw Lyssa being lifted into the air. A Slayer on horseback took her up behind him and urged his mount toward the open gate. Colwyn shouted to her again, but this time could not tell if she heard his words of encouragement.

As he tried to divide his attention between Lyssa and his father, a burst of fire from one of the strange weapons struck him in the shoulder. He staggered, fell backward on the steps. His last conscious thoughts were of father and betrothed, his last sight that of the night sky indifferent above him.

There was peace, but it brought him no comfort.

The old man hid behind the tree as the ranks of mounted Slayers galloped past. Never before had the Slayers attacked a major fortress. And the White Castle at that! Truly, Ynyr thought, the Beast spends his minions freely tonight.

Strange things were adrift on the ether this night. There had been signs for weeks now. They had brought him down from his mountaintop aerie.

Amidst the hysteria of battle, his calm advice would have been useless. Now he could only pick his way sadly toward the ruined gate of the castle, the white flash of the princess's dress a warning flag weaving through his thoughts.

They would have to go after her, of course. The marriage ceremony had not been completed. There hadn't been enough time before the Slayers had made their abduction. It wasn't going to be easy.

No sentry challenged him from atop the battlements as he approached. Inside the courtyard was the stillness of death.

Only the torches still lived, shining their pallid glow on the bodies of the fallen.

Ynyr began to search, patient and resigned. If Colwyn had perished together with the others, then he might as well return to his little cabin in the mountains, for there would be no reason for pursuing this night's work.

When he finally did locate the form he'd been searching for, he was surprised and pleased to find warm air still issuing from between parted lips. Alive, then. That was something. There was still a chance.

Fumbling within his pouch, he removed several containers of ointment. Mixing them carefully, he applied the resultant ooze to the wound on the prince's left side, then applied bandaging. As he worked his ministrations, he was thinking how next to proceed. Enlightenment eluded him. Much would depend on the will of this young man lying unconscious before him.

Colwyn finally mumbled, sat up as if shot. "Lyssa!"

"She is alive, my fortunate young friend. Alive and, insofar as I could tell, unhurt. Which is more than can be said for you."

"Where?" Colwyn tried to see past the mounded corpses.

"Lie still. Beyond your immediate reach, I am afraid, though if we proceed carefully and plan well, perhaps not beyond your final one."

"*Where?*" He winced and his hand went to the back of his head.

"As I said. Out of touch, for now."

"The Slayers do not fight like men."

"And why should they, since they are not men? Expect no humanity from a Slayer. And consider yourself fortunate. When I finally found you lying amidst this slaughter I thought you dead."

"Lyssa is among *them*. There is no fortune in that. They have stolen my life."

"Then we must set to work to get it back."

"Yes, if we—" He hesitated, squinting up at his healer. "Who are you?"

"I am called Ynyr."

"I've heard of you."

"Even in far Turold?"

"The wise men of my court have spoken your name."

"And what do they say of me?"

"Many strange things."

The old man merely smiled. "You may sit up if you feel you can manage it."

With the old man's support Colwyn did so, swaying slightly for a moment, then holding his position without help.

"You took quite a blow," Ynyr told him. "But the wound looked worse than it was. You have lost some blood but not as much as you might. Had you been struck an inch more to the left . . ."

Colwyn felt the place where the Slayer's spear had struck. "So much healing so quickly."

Ynyr glanced away. "I have some small skill. But you must ride carefully for a while lest the wound reopen."

"You've come down from your home in the Granite Mountains. What for? Why choose now to abandon your hermitage?"

"I am needed now."

"For what?"

Ynyr swept a hand toward the carnage that already was beginning to fester around them. "Events have been put in motion that I had hoped to avoid dealing with for some time yet. It seems that an old man is not permitted to set his own schedules. So I am compelled to risk all to put things right again."

Colwyn's gaze took in the courtyard and the intermingled corpses. The sight of so much death in one place did much to restore his wits.

"There are no others alive?"

Ynyr shook his head. "I have seen none, though others may have had better luck. It is difficult to believe that all who fought have perished."

Colwyn's mind locked on a single, blustering image. "Father . . ." He pulled free of Ynyr's restraining hands and stood. "Father!"

Bodies were roughly shoved aside as he began searching the human debris. Ynyr followed closely, impatient but understanding. There was still much boy in this man, upon whom so much depended.

In death there is little to distinguish king from commoner. It took some time before the pale bewhiskered face of Turold yielded to his son's search. The King of Turold still held his sword tightly in his clenched right hand.

A flash of light on metal caught Colwyn's sorrowing eye. He reached down and recovered the source of the glint. It was the royal Turoldian medallion his father always wore, displaying the arms of the kingdom and the ever-present image of the ancient glaive, symbol of old power. He stared at it, glad to have something to gaze upon other than the face of his father.

A soft but insistent voice sounded behind him: "There is no time now for grief. Sorrow is a luxury reserved for those of small import. Those with destinies to fulfill must have a care how they ration their time."

"Don't speak to me in profundities, old man!" Colwyn's tone was bitter, the pain at the back of his head replaced by a much stronger one deep inside. "You haven't lost a father and a bride on the same day!"

"Nor have I ever become a king on that day."

Colwyn tried to laugh, could not. The hurt was too deep for irony. Instead, he gestured toward the courtyard and its ranked bodies and adopted a mocking voice: "How fortunate for you. I would gladly trade all I have. A kingdom? I have no kingdom."

"Your kingdom may be greater than you know."

Colwyn ignored the old man as he played with the medallion. How often as a child he'd watched it shine on his father's chest, had played with it while sitting on Turold's lap. Now its beauty seemed false, its design devoid of meaning.

"Your importunings tire me, old man. They have nothing to do with me. As for my 'kingdom,' such as it may be, I give it to you, and welcome to it."

Ynyr shook his head sadly and looked disappointed. "I came to find a king and I find a boy instead."

"Taunt me all you wish. I don't care. I would rather play the child now. Only a man can feel the hurt that deadens me inside. I long for the innocence of childhood." He turned away, angry at everything including himself, wiping the tears from his eyes. They were not replaced. He could not lose himself in sorrow because there was something remaining to him, for all that it seemed at that moment no more than a faint hope.

"Lyssa . . ."

III

Ynyr let him think a few moments longer before speaking again. "These are not the thoughts of a boy you are thinking, Colwyn. You could not play the child even if you wished. Another calls out to you, another is depending on you."

"What will they do with her?" he whispered.

"Take her to the Black Fortress."

"How can you be certain? Can you read the mind of a Slayer?"

"It is their only home, if such it can be called. The Slayers are servants. Booty belongs to masters, not servants. Aye, they will go to the Fortress."

"Can you lead me to it?" He moved to stand close to the old man. "Lead me to its door and I will make the Slayers regret the day they came to the White Castle!"

"Bold words, brave intentions, no forethought. It will do you no good to find the Fortress and the princess, only to die there instead of here. Do not be so reckless, Prince of

43

Turold–Eirig. Planning can be as useful in battle as the sharpest sword. You must have help.''

Colwyn turned away from him, his gaze peering beyond the shattered gate to the open plain beyond. The distances beckoned him.

''There is no help to be found here and I cannot spare the time to return to Turold.''

''Granted this is so.''

''Then I must find some men on the way.''

''They had best be exceptional men, to follow even a king to the Black Fortress. You ask much of those you have not even met.''

''I have no choice. I cannot imagine what lies in store for my Lyssa save that it is certain to be unpleasant in the extreme. I will not linger here while she remains in the hands of those who would do her ill. She would do the same for me were our situations reversed.''

''Indeed? Are you then so sure of your bride-to-be, whom you have met only for the briefest of moments?''

''I am sure, old man. Never have I ever been so sure of anyone, not even my father.''

There is still a chance, then, Ynyr thought gratefully. The bond has not been sealed, but at least the parts have been positioned. It is worth risking lives for.

''In the Fortress you will have to face more than the Slayers. You will face the Beast, who is their master. I have yet to meet the soldier ready to accept such a challenge. I expect it from a king-to-be, but not from any common man-at-arms.''

''Then we will have to find uncommon men, won't we? As to the question of how we will deal with the Beast, leave me to worry on that. He lives, and anything that lives can die. I have studied much of statecraft and much of war, and have learned that there are no absolutes to either. He is not immortal. Strength does not mean invulnerability.''

"Spoken like a king!" said Ynyr delightedly. Yes, the young prince was ready. Ynyr now gave himself wholeheartedly over to the dangerous enterprise.

"Perhaps he *can* be slain, but no man has ever seen him and lived. You will need more power than lies in uncommon men or swords, more than even the combined armies of Eirig and Turold could provide . . . though it would be comforting to have an army with us. Still,"—he shrugged knowingly— "one fights with what weapons one can muster.''

"I am willing to make use of any suggestions you might have, old man. What weapons do you speak of?''

Ynyr spoke complacently, as though by the mere act of doing so he could make the extraordinary sound commonplace.

"There is the original from which the symbol on your father's medallion derives.''

Colwyn glanced reflexively down at the metal circlet. "The arms of the first kingdom of Turold?''

"No, Colwyn. Think on what I have just said.''

He frowned, then a look of amazement came over his face. "What, *the* glaive? You are crazy, old man! Or a fool. Go back to your hut and do not toy with my anger. I will find the Black Fortress by myself and assail it as best I am able. I have some poor skills, but I strive not to include absurdity among them.''

"But uncertainty remains. I see it in your face. Come with me, Prince of Krull, and we shall see who is the fool.'' He turned and picked his way across the graveyard, there to mount a riderless horse and send it trotting toward the gate.

Colwyn hesitated, then slipped the chain and medallion over his neck and hurried to find a mount with which to follow. Surely the old man was mad, but he had been well-thought-of by the scholars responsible for Colwyn's education. Mystery surrounded his name, but always accompanied by veneration.

Was it possible for wise men to venerate a fool? There was little time to wonder. With a curse he secured a horse and followed in Ynyr's wake. Even an old, foolish ally was better than none. Until better choices presented themselves, he could do worse than listen to the advice of the one man willing to aid him in his search. Whatever his other abilities, Colwyn had to admit that this Ynyr did not quake in terror at the mere mention of the Beast's name. That counted for something.

The mountains Ynyr led Colwyn into were strange to him, their composition different from those of Turold. From these granite blocks had been cut the foundation of the White Castle. He hoped they would be of more help than those easily breeched walls had been.

Here resided strange creatures that were only rumor in far-off Turold: trees that put their heads into the earth and thrust flailing roots at a yawning sky; little furry things with too many eyes; and hard-shelled monsters that disguised themselves with flowers and herbs.

Here also resided Ynyr, be he wise man or fool. At least he seemed to know where he was going. The winding course he chose was as good a road as any to Colwyn, so long as it led eventually to the Black Fortress and his beloved. The medallion bounced coldly against his chest.

He fingered it absently as he spoke. "The glaive is nothing but an ancient symbol. I was taught in school that symbols are distorted representations of half-remembered realities. It doesn't actually exist."

"Oh, it exists." Ynyr pointed toward a confluence of tall peaks. "Up there. You are partially right, though. It is ancient."

"I need weapons, not symbols." Colwyn directed his horse

around a huge boulder, keeping his attention on the ground
ahead. The rock here was broken and slippery. He would be
glad when they came to firmer ground.

"Do not be so quick to disdain the use of symbols, my
boy. They have their uses. Once, the glaive was more than a
symbol. It was a powerful device, a great weapon. In the
right hands it can be so again."

"In my hands?"

"I wish I knew for certain. I have studied long hours alone
and have learned much from our history."

"Tell me."

"Not now. This is not the time or place. When it is time I
will tell you. Before you can learn the secrets of the past, you
must secure the future. For now it is enough for you to know
that only a true prince of the mind can successfully make use
of the glaive."

Colwyn frowned. "Prince of the mind? I'm not sure that I
understand."

"Recall your marriage ceremony. Yes, I know it is painful,
but recall. The passing of fire to water is proof that certain
abilities have been inculcated in you, among them the ability
to utilize your mind in ways alien to the average man."

"That's a prince's right."

"No, boy, it is *not* a prince's right! There's much more to
it than that. Some day I hope to make you realize how much
more." His attention turned from Colwyn to a saddle between
two crags. "We are near."

"If you are so sensitive to such things, and to this glaive
you insist is no fairy tale, and to the knowledge that sur-
rounds it, why do you not wield it yourself against the
Slayers?"

Ynyr smiled ruefully. "It is true I am master of much that
would startle you. But it is equally true there are things I

cannot do. Employing the glaive properly is among them.
And there is still an additional restraint.''

''What might that be?''

''I am old, Colwyn. Sad as it is, there are times when
knowledge and talent must be supplemented with muscle. I
might possibly have made use of the glaive many years ago,
but no longer. And at that time Krull was at peace and there
was no reason to wield it.''

''Are you so sure that I am the right one?'' Sudden
responsibility weighed heavily on Colwyn. He was beginning
to believe in this old man. ''Maybe you are mistaken in
choosing me for this task.''

''Perhaps. Nothing is certain,'' Ynyr told him with unsettling
candor. ''We'll know soon enough.'' He reined in his horse
and let Colwyn take the lead. The prince looked back.

''No, boy, I can't go with you. This far and no farther. I
would endanger us both by accompanying you farther.''

''Then rest here, old man, and ease your mind. I'll come
back with it. If there's anything up there''—he nodded toward
the higher slopes, where a wind of hollow voice beckoned
mournfully—''to come back with.''

''Oh, it's up there all right,'' Ynyr assured him somberly
as he dismounted. There was a far-off look in his eyes as he
squinted up at the silent rocks. ''It's up there, and if you do
not come back with it, you will not come back at all.'' His
gaze shifted back to Colwyn. ''I am not trying to frighten
you. Other men have sought the power of the glaive and have
left only bold promises as epitaphs. Be sure of yourself.''

The prince's tone was bitter. ''Do I have a choice?''

''You do. No one else does. You are Krull's last option.''

''And Lyssa's. Wait here for me, Ynyr.'' He chucked the
reins, urging his horse upward.

Eventually the slope sharpened to such a degree that he had
to leave his mount behind. Soon he found himself above the

treeline, where only the wind grows. It blew sharply into his face, informing him that he was a trespasser in this rarefied region and that his continued existence came at the whim of the elements. He was hiking the land of quick storms and brutal cold, a place where a man's life was as fragile as the lichen and grass that clung to the rocks. In a few months this whole country would sleep beneath many feet of snow.

Better not to linger here, then, he told himself, forcing his legs to work harder. Anger pushed him from behind, determination drew him from ahead. His thoughts were full of Lyssa and of Ynyr's strange talk.

He was not so preoccupied that he failed to hear the ominous rumbling from above.

The first rocks were mere pebbles, advance scouts for the avalanche to come. The falling stones rapidly became bigger. One just missed crushing his right leg. Frantically he dodged as he sought with his eyes for a place of safety, but the bare, rocky slope was devoid of shelter.

When in doubt, attack, his father had always told him. Instead of trying to flee he held his ground and met each threat while facing it, dodging skillfully. Soon the landslide had to end. He wouldn't let it halt his ascent.

When the last boulder had slid harmlessly past, to crash somewhere on the slopes far below, he rested only a moment to catch his breath before pulling his way upward once again. The terrain grew steeper and ever more precipitous but, mindful of Ynyr's words, he pressed on, keeping his eyes always on the crags above.

When it seemed he must step out onto the sky itself he reached a dark stain in the sheer cliffs. The stain marked a cleft in the rocks. Steam rose from within, emerging from the belly of the mountain in fitful, uncertain puffs.

What did you expect? he asked himself. To find the glaive resting on a golden cushion out in the open, just waiting for

you to pick up and slip into your belt? Cautiously, he started
into the hissing crevice.

The narrow break in the rock led into the mountain,
working its way gently downward. There were false side
passages and one place where he had to brace his back
against one wall and his feet against the other to shinny
down. The chimney opened into a small cave. Steam beaded
his face and tickled his throat.

There was water here, and stone that ran like red milk,
glowing and bubbling merrily near the back of the cavern.
Every time a pool of water overflowed onto the molten rock a
burst of superheated steam shot ceilingward. Shielding his
face, he worked his way toward the back, nearly tripping over
a rock.

Except that it wasn't a rock. It was rounder and whiter than
the exfoliated fragments he'd stumbled over on the slope
outside, and it displayed gaps that had once housed human
senses. The skull was also badly charred. He stared at it
somberly. Evidently there were occasions when this cavern
was less than hospitable. Though it was incapable of threatening
him, he edged around it. There were times when the dead
could surprise you by fighting back.

Several pieces of ceiling collapsed into the lava basin. He
turned away fast, but not quickly enough to avoid the splash
of molten material. The several droplets that struck him
burned holes in his tunic and he spent a frantic moment
beating out the tiny fires.

Keeping himself poised for another rapid retreat, he bent
over the bubbling pool. It was thick and shone a bright orange
red; yet he thought he could make out something darker lying
in the depths. The object was long and narrow, thicker at one
end than the other.

He searched the floor of the cavern. There was nothing as
useful as a tree limb, and he could imagine how long the

bones of his unlucky predecessor would last if thrust into that hellish vat. He found a broken stalagtite, returned to the pool and reached with it toward the dark shape. The shape moved, confirming his judgment. There was no chance to raise it clear of the lava with the stalagtite. The limestone was already melting away in his hand.

He dropped it and considered how to proceed as he watched it dissolve. The pit continued to boil and froth. There was a distant rumble, as though the mountain were growing impatient with him.

Remember your marriage ceremony, Ynyr had instructed him. Colwyn trembled a little at the prospect thus raised, but it was clear there was only one way he could proceed.

He thought back to the ceremony, worked to assume again the requisite mental posture. Only this time, he had to prove himself to a far less forgiving bride than Lyssa. It should not take long. He would not have long. There could be no uncertainty, no hesitation. Half closing his eyes, he thoughtfully rolled his right sleeve up to the shoulder.

Then he gritted his teeth and plunged his bare right hand into the seething cauldron.

There was no pain. Only a faint tingling, an odd sensation as full of excitement as threat. His arm felt through the molten rock for only a few seconds. Then he yanked it out, blinking in wonder at the object he'd retrieved.

The flattened, starlike glaive sported five curved arms in which blades lay concealed. It was a dull black from years of sleeping untouched in the lava basin. So intent was he on the glaive itself, on this fragment of mythology suddenly become real in his hand, that he ignored the flames that enveloped his arm.

Abruptly the dancing fire vanished into the glaive, sucked up by some unheard call. As it disappeared, the black crust of chilled lava cracked from the surface. Now Colwyn was compelled to turn his eyes aside as the black became gold and the glaive began to burn with a light as strong as the sun's.

Flat and made to fit the hand, it seemed as natural to fling it as it was unnatural to see it return to his hand. His exuberance sent him scrambling and sliding back down the mountainside, and it was as much luck as good sense that enabled him to reach the waiting Ynyr unhurt.

"I have it, Ynyr, I have it! The glaive *is* real, and I am its master!" He raised the weapon and made as if to throw it over the steep slopes, but Ynyr hurried to forestall him.

"What's wrong? This *is* the glaive you spoke of, isn't it? I saw no other weapon."

Ynyr eyed him thoughtfully. "And what else could it be? Yes, that's the glaive of legend, as surely as we both stand here examining it."

Colwyn frowned. "Then, what troubles you? Haven't I come safely back with it?"

"You have acquired power, yes. Wisdom is far more elusive and harder to come by. Power used frivolously is power wasted." He nodded toward the gleaming weapon. "I am pleased, but not awed."

This time Colwyn disdained a quick reply in favor of a moment's hard thought, which pleased Ynyr considerably. The prince slipped the glaive into a loop on his belt.

"That's better," said Ynyr. "You're learning. Don't use the glaive until you need it. Then the power will be there when you require it most. It is not a toy. Do not play with it, Colwyn."

"How will I know when to use it?"

"That is easier known than when not to." He peered closely at the glaive with old eyes, ran the fingers of one hand over its five golden arms. It was cold to his touch, inanimate now, responsive only to Colwyn's commands. The old books described it accurately, he thought. It shone as though it had been forged yesterday. Now if only the descriptions of its powers were equally accurate.

If this young prince will grow up, there may yet be a chance to drive the Slayers and their master from the world. It is much to place on the shoulders of one so headstrong and inexperienced. At least he is willing to take advice, Ynyr mused. That was a hopeful sign.

"You will know," he told him confidently.

Colwyn was looking past him, across the mountain's flanks down to the forested hills beyond. Power was in his hand and revenge in his heart. He felt there was nothing that could stand against him. It remained for Ynyr to worry about what lay in the impetuous prince's head.

"Lead me to the Black Fortress and I'll use it soon enough," Colwyn muttered angrily. He hefted the glaive, luxuriating in its solidity and coldness. "It strains to be used and I terribly want to use it."

"Patience, patience. Finding the Fortress is not easy. It knows no single kingdom but claims all Krull as its domain. With each sunrise the Fortress moves. Sometimes it comes to rest in the mountains, othertimes the desert, sometimes it hovers over the sea. Never twice in the same place. Even the Beast does not control everything, so he moves about to confuse and frustrate as well as to terrify. Furthermore, he is dependent for such movement on the activity of Krull's magnetosphere, which is in a constant state of flux."

Colwyn looked baffled. "Old man, you use words I do not know."

"Ancient words, Colwyn."

"It is Lyssa I seek. You told me you knew where to find the Fortress."

"Courage is not the only virtue of a king, nor is the power he may hold in his hand. Courtesy is also useful, especially toward one's elders. You would not be here now nor that,"

—he gestured to the glaive—"be in your possession if not for me."

Colwyn forced himself to relax. "I'm sorry. It's only that the thought of Lyssa . . . *there* . . ."

"Such thinking crowds reason from your brain and weakens you. You need more than resolve to reach and penetrate the Fortress. Stealth is less exhausting than strength. Spend the former wisely and husband the latter." Colwyn's inner torment was plain to see and Ynyr softened his tone, put a comforting hand on the prince's shoulder.

"I do have a tendency to lecture, I know. It's only that more than Lyssa's fate rides with us on this journey, my boy. I know how you are feeling. I too was young once. I too have loved as you do." His voice fell. "But you will be luckier than I. You must be."

Come now, old man, he told himself angrily, this is no time to burden the lad with your own sordid past. What he needs now is advice and reassurance.

"What I told you, Colwyn, was that I knew *how* to find the Fortress. That is not the same as knowing where it is today. You hold in your hands one device of the ancients. Krull holds other secrets. The way we will locate the Fortress is by enlisting the aid of the Emerald Seer."

"But his whereabouts are a mystery to all."

"Not quite all," Ynyr corrected him. "It is known to me. Oh, don't look so startled. Did you think that having solved one mystery,"—and he pointed to the glaive—"I was incapable of solving any more? A day's journey from here lies the means by which a man may extend his vision. Come."

"If it lies within a day's ride of the White Castle, why has the place never been found before?"

Ynyr shook his head. So much to teach, so little time for instruction. "The glaive lay in a spot even nearer and had done so undisturbed for hundreds of years. Proximity is not

the same thing as being close at hand. The Emerald Seer
guards his privacy with more subtlety.''

Colwyn thought back to the charred skull he'd stumbled
over in the cavern of the glaive and nodded slowly. He mulled
over the old man's words as they started down the mountain.

IV

Their journey took them through a mountain pass rarely traversed by the citizens of Eirig. Soon they once more enjoyed the company of evergreens and berry bushes. Birds and insects filled the airways between the trees, reminding Colwyn that he belonged to the world of the living. Yet the serenity of the forest was deceiving. He knew that at any instant it could be crushed to pulp at the Beast's whim, as could any part of Krull.

They followed a stream downhill, stopping beside a low bank where the water slowed and dozed, forming a small pool. Ynyr dismounted and went to draw himself a drink while his companion fiddled with the glaive. Like any sensible outrider, Colwyn carried leather strips and clamps for repairing horse tack or boots while on the road. Now he utilized them to fashion a carrying strap and protective pouch for the glaive so he could carry it slung from his belt. He did not trust it to the saddlebags and there might come a time when having it close at hand could save a life.

As the pouch neared completion, a peculiar aroma caught his attention. He sniffed. Nearby, the tethered horses stirred uneasily. Something singed the evening air. His eyes widened as something spun widly past him, causing him to duck instinctively. Ynyr merely looked interested.

At first Colwyn thought it might be a hare or some other small game thrown aside by a hidden predator. He was positive he saw the face of a fox in the whirling shape. Or were those deer legs? Elk antlers, the hind end of a steer, and the startled face of a globus all mixed together, spinning round and round with human limbs and features.

Eventually this aerial confusion came to rest with a violent splash. The smell and sound vanished and he found himself standing next to the pool, confronting a young man of small stature. The visitor lay facedown in the pool, kicking and flailing at the water.

"Help, help, I'm drowning!"

Colwyn leaned forward, resting his right arm on his thigh as he studied the new arrival. "I doubt it. The water you're lying in is barely a foot deep."

At this the stranger ceased his exertions and rolled over. He sat upright and wiped at the mud on his shirt, muttering to himself. His hair was stringy and long and his attitude as tart as pickled herring. Slowly he rose, still striving to divest himself of the grime so recently and ignominiously acquired.

"Well, it could have been quicksand. I might have been dragged down to my death while you stood there gawking. That is not the reaction of a friend." He waded soggily out of the pool, kicking first one leg and then the other, like a dog trying to shed water. He eyed his surroundings warily.

"Where is this place?"

"A forest near the foothills of the Granite Mountains, on the far side from the kingdom of Eirig–Turold."

The little man frowned at him. "Now, I know of the kingdom of Eirig, and I've heard of far Turold, but of Eirig–Turold I know nothing."

"There has been a merging made. The kingdoms have been joined."

"I am underwhelmed. The Granite Mountains, you say?" Colwyn nodded. "Blast and frog jumps! A thousand miles off course!" He shrugged sadly. "Well, I was rushed. There was a certain difference of opinion concerning a gooseberry trifle. The foolish man left it sitting isolated and friendless on his windowsill, poor thing. What did he expect?"

"Perhaps," Colwyn speculated, "he expected to eat it."

The stranger glared at Colwyn. "For that rudeness, lout, you're going to spend the rest of your life as a toad. Or would you rather be a frog? No, I'd say toad-dom would fit that face better." He hesitated, eyed Colwyn cautiously. "Well, aren't you going to quake in fear? Aren't you going to go to your knees to beg my forgiveness?"

Colwyn sighed, shook his head and turned away from the pool. "Not right now. There's a fire to attend to and the question of supper. Other matters to be dealt with."

"Other matters? I'll show you what matters need attending to!" Rummaging through his numerous pockets he yanked out small scraps of multicolored paper filled with indecipherable scribbling. He settled on one scrap, squinting at it.

"No, that's a recipe for a hot fudge sauce." He moved to throw it aside, thought better of it, and shoved it back into a pocket. "Well, a goose will have to do. Warmer than a toad, but I can't waste time when I'm mad. Better to work when one's in the mood. Yes, a goose, fat and ugly!"

There were certainly many words inscribed on the piece of paper and some of them were very long and difficult. The visitor stumbled over their pronunciation more than once. Finally he concluded his invocation on a rising inflection and snapped his fingers at Colwyn.

Colwyn turned and regarded the goose squatting at the water's edge with interest. No doubt about it, this stranger had talent. Somewhat erratic, however. He laughed.

"Very fat and very ugly. I should not have doubted you."

The goose let out an angry honk, seemed befuddled at the noise, and made a dash at Colwyn. It halted short of its target, apparently thinking better of the idea, and turned instead to waddle across to where a slip of paper rested by the pool's bank. It cocked a querulous eye at it, obviously in a fowl temper, and honked steadily and softly.

A white cloud enveloped it. Colwyn amused himself by trying to decide whether it revealed more goose than visitor. The cloud resolved the argument by disappearing with a soft popping sound, leaving the stranger behind. If naught else, the effort had cleaned him up a little.

He sounded only slightly chastened. "And from that you see what I could have done to you if I were a vengeful man." More softly he muttered, "Blasted matter transformations use so blasted much energy a body can't tell whether he's coming or going." He put a hand to his forehead.

"I am tired. Leave me now, lest a worse fate befall thee."

Colwyn finished putting out the fire and packed the last of his belongings. Ynyr waited patiently nearby, eyeing their intemperate guest with curiosity. Matter transformation was a difficult business. The little fellow was both adept and inept.

"We intend to take our leave of this campsite, but the forest is not safe. You'd best travel with us."

The stranger pulled himself up to his full height and glared imperiously at Colwyn. "Me? Travel with *you*? Do you know who I am? Do you have the faintest idea, lout, in whose presence you stand?"

Colwyn leaned against his horse. "No, but I have this odd feeling you're going to tell me."

Either the visitor was beyond sarcasm or else simply chose to ignore it. "I am Ergo the Magnificent; short in stature, tall in power, narrow of purpose, wide of vision." This was delivered with appropriately descriptive gestures. "And I do not travel with peasants and beggars. Good day to you." Whereupon he whirled and strode purposefully (though, insofar as Colwyn could see, aimlessly) into the woods.

He repressed a chuckle as he mounted. Ynyr pulled himself into his own saddle.

"He'll be the first member of our army."

Ynyr frowned, looked back over a shoulder. "Of what use could he be?"

"He is the master of a talent. Well, not a master, perhaps, but matter transformation is a tricky business."

"Indeed it is, my boy, but if casually handled it can be more dangerous than useful. I do not like to see such power indifferently employed."

"I seem to have heard that recently," said Colwyn with a grin. "But if such power confuses the one who employs it, think how it would confuse his enemies!"

"Confusion benefits no one, least of all us."

"I defer to you in matters of history and learning, Ynyr, but where combat is concerned I have studied long and hard under dedicated instructors. When assaulting an enemy of greater strength, confusion can be a potent ally. Besides which, he seems to be a man of spirit as well as spirits. Give me a fighter with steel in his backbone and I'll not concern myself with the composition of his sword. This one would stand by a friend."

"If he has any."

"True enough. He does strike me as the obstreperous sort. I've seen his kind before, though. When they are unsure of their position, they feel it's best to strike out and see what their surroundings are made of."

"Have a care, Colwyn, that he does not accidentally strike at you."

"I'll be careful. Meanwhile, let's try and have patience with him, should he change his mind and rejoin us. Perhaps his instructor in alchemical matters was an indifferent one. Could you help him perfect his useful art?"

"I'm afraid my knowledge is of more practical matters. I do not dabble in arcane arts. But my opinion of this one," —and he gestured back across the pool—"is that in an awkward situation he'd most likely transform himself into a crow and fly like mad for the nearest place of safety."

"I think you do him an injustice. Still, there might be opportunities to test him further along the way."

Ynyr still stared back at where the forest was swallowing up the campsite. "No doubt there might be. *If* he rejoins us."

It was very quiet in the woods. Much quieter than the town from which Ergo the Magnificent had so recently and hastily beat a retreat. The moon hung faint and bilious in the lowing sky, hardly lifting the spirits of the trees surrounding him. Indeed, with each step he took, their branches seemed to bend a little lower, reaching toward him with stiff, sharp fingers. Dead leaves and toadstools crunched beneath his feet, and night murmurs assaulted his hearing. He longed for the bright lights and cheerful cries of Moukaskar, the city he'd fled. He would even have paid for the rifled trifle.

There—a noise, off to his left! A rabbit or some other evening forager, he assured himself. Harmless as the wind. The sound came a second time and he stopped to peer close. Saints and devils, was that an eye? A cold sweat broke out on the back of his neck. It surely was an awfully big eye. Much too big for a rabbit. It grew even larger as it moved suddenly toward him.

Then in the moonlight he saw a beardless face, and the source of the solitary stare was apparent. It was solitary because that face held but a single eye.

He was too startled to cry out, but not too startled to whirl and break into a desperate sprint. Branches and leaves seemed determined to restrain him as he tore back toward the pool, retracing his steps in a third the time while glancing repeatedly back over his shoulder. The single eye vanished, outdistanced by his mad flight. Or perhaps it had reasons for not pursuing.

He burst into the clearing bordering the stream and looked frantically about. No sign of the two men who'd witnessed his inglorious arrival. In panic he splashed through the water, crossing the stream where it narrowed again beneath the pool. Ah, there, just ahead! Movement among the bushes and the comforting sound of horses' hooves.

As he grew near he thought to slow to a stately walk and compose himself.

"Why, if it isn't Ergo the Magnificent. And the Breathless. Something give you a start?" Colwyn looked past the smaller man, back into the forest. He saw nothing.

"Nonsense," Ergo replied haughtily. "Ergo the Magnificent is not frightenable."

"Nor does he talk very well when he's out of breath. You are sweating, my friend."

"My evening exercise. I never miss it."

"I see," Colwyn turned his attention back to the trail ahead. "Then what brings you so soon into our company again?"

"I just remembered that I have some urgent business in this direction."

"I daresay, from the way you're breathing." He reached a hand toward the other man. Ergo hesitated, then took the offer and swung himself up onto the horse behind Colwyn. "What business might that be?"

"Staying alive," Ergo confessed, glancing nervously behind them. Whatever creature it belonged to, the eye stayed mercifully hidden.

Colwyn chuckled. "Then it seems we are in the same business, my friend. And men who work the same business ought to stick together."

"Most assuredly," agreed Ergo quickly.

Lyssa had never thought of a nightmare as having walls and a floor, a ceiling and strangely hued hidden lights. A nightmare was thin and wispy, faint and impalpable. It ought not to ring hollowly beneath one's shoes or to twist and turn like the thoughts of an evil courtier.

Was she inside the Black Fortress or inside her own mind? She clung precariously to her sanity as she rushed down weaving, convoluted corridors that seemed spun of gold and ceramic instead of honest wood or stone. She could not imagine how such a place could have been built. Perhaps it had not been built in the sense men thought of as "built." Perhaps it had been grown, for certain of the tunnels and cavernous hallways she raced through resembled far more the inside of some stolid, immobile creature than the corridors of any building ever described to her in her lessons.

Occasionally a wall would ooze shut behind her, forcing her onward, or a tall white Slayer would appear to block her path. Then she would turn desperately down any unblocked passageway, her dress whirling around her legs, seeking even temporary freedom.

Freedom: it was little more than an intellectual exercise, since it was clear that even if she stumbled across the right tools she'd be unable to dig herself to freedom. But it was a useful abstract to concentrate on as she ran, and it helped to keep her from going mad.

She thought also of Colwyn and the burning fresh love that had drawn them so close so quickly, saw him buried under a wave of Slayers as he'd tried to hack his way through to her in the castle courtyard. What must he be thinking of her now? Would he be more at peace believing her still alive, with a chance for rescue, or better off thinking her dead?

No matter. She had no way of conveying a message to him. Her palm burned as she thought of him and she remembered the gentle, comforting heat of the flame she'd taken from the font during the ceremony. It gave her strength, that memory. Strength to keep hoping, strength to run on.

Once, a gown resplendent with jewels and metallic thread appeared like a vision before her. Above it floated a crown of precious metal and strange mien. It held her transfixed with its beauty for a long moment, until she saw the threat that lay beyond. To some it might appear raiment fit for a queen but Lyssa was far more perceptive than that. It was beautiful, yes, but so were many burial shrouds.

She turned from it and rushed on.

There were too many dead trees around for Colwyn's liking. They'd reached a defile in the rocks, a place of desolation and broken stone. At least the morning fog had dissipated. Walls without substance, his father had once called such fogs. The mark of difficult country.

The sun hung somewhere overhead, masked by the sheer walls that rose around them. Birds and other less wholesome things called out hesitantly, as though uncertain of safety. Lonely sounds fit for a lonely place. He would be glad when they had passed beyond.

Something nudged him in the small of the back and he felt

his passenger shifting position. Ergo sat behind the saddle and by now it must be wearying to him.

"How are you doing back there, my magnificent little friend?"

"Not magnificently, I fear. I have spent all morning debating the benefits of riding thus versus walking. My feet opt for their present status but another part of me disagrees most strenuously."

"I'm sorry. When we reach a town we'll have to see about acquiring a mount for you."

"With what? I left my last place of residence in such a rush that I was compelled to leave the bulk of my fortune behind."

"It's your help I need, not your money. I am willing to help those who help me."

Ergo perked up, the soreness that attended his fundament temporarily forgotten. "You have money, then?"

"Enough to provide you with a horse, anyway." That told Ergo little, which was precisely what Colwyn wanted him to know.

Ergo peered around his companion's side, raised his voice. "You are not a great chooser of roads, old man."

"Our road has been chosen for us," Ynyr replied importantly.

"I was referring to that which passes beneath our horses' hooves, not that which conveys our spirits."

"As you prefer," said Ynyr. "To place your question on a less exhalted plain, this particular *road* avoids the most dangerous bogs and marshlands while saving us half a day of travel. No highways lead to our current destination. I should think that, given your present seat, you would be particularly appreciative of any time saved."

Ergo's muttered reply was somewhat less than grateful.

The canyon narrowed further and Colwyn's unease intensified as it did so.

"Ynyr, shouldn't we be out of these rocks by now? It seems we've been riding through them for ages."

"I'm sorry, my boy, but this is the only way to avoid the marshlands. Rest easy. We'll emerge into more open country soon enough."

They rode on. With a sensitive portion of his anatomy continuing to shout its protests, Ergo finally descended to give his feet some exercise, walking alongside Colwyn's horse. Through sleepy eyes quickly opened he thought he saw a half-solid shape behind the rocks. A man could see anything he wanted to in such a place. Here the boulders became a sculpted horse, there a ship far out at sea, there a man's contorted face, there another . . . and another.

He stared wide-eyed at the jumble of rocks on either side of the path they trod. Another face appeared briefly alongside the last. It wasn't like stone to repeat its illusions so often or so faithfully. He moved close to the horse and his voice became an anxious whisper.

"Robbers! On both sides, Colwyn."

"I've been watching them." Colwyn's reply was calm. "They've been paralleling us for several minutes now, choosing their spot. Restrain yourself. They're only men. We don't know for sure that they're robbers. You leap to conclusions."

"I would gladly leap there if I thought it a safer place. Faces as ugly as those I've seen could only belong to robbers. What do you think such men are about, hiding themselves in this kind of country? Picking berries?" Aware of the fear in his voice he hastened to cover it with bravado.

"Well, not to worry. I'll turn them all into pigs. Now, where did I put that porcine formulation?" He started rummaging through his slips of paper.

Two men rose from opposite sides of the trail, flung their massive axes toward him simultaneously. Each ax blade locked itself over his neck, their weight pinning the unfortunate Ergo to the ground.

"That does it!" he yelled from where he lay, struggling with the pinioning blades. He was more angry now than frightened. "You'll oink and squeal for the rest of your lives!"

Unfortunately, the only pig that appeared near the trail found itself neatly trapped beneath the interlocking ax handles. It oinked and squealed with considerable vigor.

Contrary to Ergo's prejudicial observation, the man who stepped clear of the rocks to confront Colwyn was not especially ugly, but it was plain for anyone to see that he hadn't lived an easy life at court, either. There were scars on his face that had not been put there by farming implements, and his expression was hard and cold. Muscles rippled beneath his shirt sleeves like snakes dreaming under leather.

"You are surrounded by a hundred men," he informed Colwyn. "Throw down your weapons and surrender your money."

Colwyn dismounted to study his challenger. "A hundred is not enough."

That brought forth an amused smile. "Well, well, what have we here? A fighter?" He looked curiously at Colwyn, then at Ynyr. "A welcome change from the usual quavering traveler. A few moments diversion, they say, is refreshing for the soul."

"I would agree with you, were I not in a hurry. If we are to talk of souls, stranger, have a care for your own, lest it find itself liberated sooner than you think. And if it's pleasurable diversion you intend, you're short about ninety men."

The man laughed good-humoredly. "Not only a fighter, but a counter too!"

A second man stepped out of the fog. His expression was sour, his attitude one of irritated boredom. He was stocky and rotund, but Colwyn could see the muscle beneath the fat. His hand held a peculiar and lethal-looking bolo.

"What is this small talk? Idle chatter is for idle men. Kill them and be done with it, Torquil."

"Softly go, Rhun." The man named Torquil was studying the nonchalant horseman cautiously. "I don't kill without reason."

"Nor do I," Colwyn assured him, eyeing the one called Rhun with unconcealed distaste. "The both of you can be thankful for that."

Rhun took a step forward, brandishing the bolo. It was designed not for bringing down fleeing fowl, but for killing.

"Interesting toy you have there, friend. Take another step toward me and you'd best be certain of its use."

The heavyset man held his ground and continued to eye Colwyn threateningly. Strong and skillful, Colwyn decided, but tending to the impetuous. The one to concentrate on was the apparent leader, Torquil.

Then he noticed something else: Torquil wore iron manacles on his wrists. In the fog it had been difficult to tell if they were wrist shields, decorative bracelets, or something else. Now he could see that the combative Rhun wore identical manacles. Several links of heavy chain dangled from one.

"You are escaped prisoners." It was not a question.

Nor did Torquil try to deny it. He grinned and gestured into the fog where the rest of his band waited. "Say rather, misunderstood citizens. Society has frowned on our actions, sir. But in essence you are correct. We are that, each and every man of us. Thieves, bandits, tax avoiders, brawlers, stealers of favors from men and women both. Vagabonds forced to eke out a living any way we can."

"Desperate men, I should say. That's quite a litany of offenses, though much was evident from first sight of you."

"Beauty is not necessary to our profession. Aye, we're as

desperate as you'll ever set eyes upon, traveler . . . which is one reason we are not to be trifled with. If you will put your hand away from that fine sword of yours, it will not be necessary for us to demonstrate to you just how desperate we can be.

"As for our appearance, I make no apologies. The life of a fugitive is constrained by circumstance, which smells pestiferously in our case. No, the only thing you can trust in is our desperation."

"Good." Colwyn moved his sword slightly, noted the slight twitch of Torquil's right hand. Fast, he thought. Fast but controlled. "Those are the kind of men I need."

"*You* need?" Torquil tried to laugh again, but he was a little confused and his heart wasn't in it. This was not the usual sort of confrontation he and his followers were accustomed to. Trembling in fear was normal. A quick hand-over of any valuables without bloodshed, that was typical. On rare occasions some fool resisted, and every such confrontation had ended in the same way.

But this stranger's casual demeanor was unsettling. It implied confidence and knowledge. It bothered Torquil. There was no sign they were preparing to flee, either.

And then there was this odd talk about followers. Torquil continued to study his confident young opponent. He certainly didn't have the look of a thief. If he was, he displayed strange taste in henchmen: one little fool full of braggadocio and one quiet old man. Odd too the way the old man seemed supremely indifferent to the whole discussion, as though the weather and the terrain ahead were more important than whatever Torquil and his band might try.

It was all very much out of the ordinary, and Torquil hadn't kept his neck intact this long by rushing blindly into inexplicable situations. His sword hand itched. He had to make a decision soon. Back in the woods Bardolph and Kegan must be fingering the triggers of their crossbows nervously, wondering at the delay. Something kept him from giving the attack signal.

In the presence of indecision, he chose to stall. He gestured toward the trees. "These men follow no man but me, and I follow no man at all. There are no men left in this world *worth* following. So I am sorry to have to decline your offer, stranger, but you'll have to seek help elsewhere. After you've handed over your money, that is."

"I do not blame you for what you say. Truly there are few men worth following. But would you not follow a king?"

Torquil squinted at the rider. Nearby Sweyn was muttering, "I grow tired of this discourse, Torquil. Let's finish them before some other garrulous fools come along and increase our risk."

"Hold your guts." He kept his eyes on Colwyn. "There are plenty of lunatics wandering the countryside claiming to be kings. We live in times that seem to encourage such idiocy. Such folk prey on the fears of the credulous. I am not credulous. Neither are my men."

"You have not answered my question: would you not follow a king?"

"Perhaps, though I've had nothing from kings but ill."

Colwyn smiled. "A common complaint, often justified. A king is often too distanced from his people. Blame him not for the occasional excesses of minor bureaucrats. Answer me, man. Would you follow a king to the Black Fortress?"

At that Torquil relaxed, smiled at Sweyn. "See? I told you. You worry too much. We've nothing to fear from these three." He turned back to Colwyn. "I confess you had me going for a while there, stranger, with your facile chatter of kings and followers. You play neat with words, but now I know that you're a lunatic. The Black Fortress!" He and Sweyn silently shared the grim joke.

"I wouldn't follow my own father to the Black Fortress, stranger. Not that he'd be fool enough to go there. Even if it could be reached, there's nothing to be found there save death and destruction, and those I can find in more manageable quantities right here. D'you think I'm as mad as you, that I'd flee civil war in order to meet a worse death than any captain of guards could mete out?"

"Is it mad," Colwyn asked softly, "to want to defend your world?"

"World? What is this talk of a 'world'? Once I had a village to call home. A warlord burned it to the ground. Now I have no home, and certainly no 'world.'"

"All Krull suffers at the hands of the Slayers."

"All Krull suffers at the hand of winter," Rhun snapped mockingly, "but we don't try to fight the seasons. We'd fare as well if we went against the Slayers."

"It's true the Slayers are different from ordinary warriors, but they are mortal. They can be slain."

"So what?" Torquil challenged him. "Kill a Slayer and ten more appear to avenge him."

"All the Slayers come from the lair of the Beast, which is the Black Fortress. Defeat the Beast and you defeat all the Slayers."

"You talk more foolishness."

"Is it foolish to fight for your homes and families? Is it foolish to fight for your children's sake? If that's not worth fighting for, what is? If these invaders conquer, you won't even keep the independence of escaped prisoners, for all men will become prisoners."

"Noble sentiments," said a new voice as its owner showed himself, "except that we fight for profit. Gold—that's worth fighting for." Murmurs of assent sounded from the rocks. Not many, Colwyn thought. Certainly far fewer than a hundred. Perhaps no more than a dozen.

"Where is the profit in your fight?" the man asked.

"The profit is freedom," Colwyn told him, "and fame."

"Freedom we have," Torquil replied, "and fame is an empty purse. Count it and go broke, eat it and go hungry, seek it and go mad. Fame is what fools yearn for and wise men shun."

Ynyr turned in his saddle and spoke for the first time. To those who had never heard the old man speak, there was a peculiarly arresting quality to his soft, cutting tone. Torquil and his followers listened in spite of themselves.

"Fame is what you leave to your children."

Torquil gaped at him, tried to see through the white-haired figure straddling the other horse. "You know nothing of me. How did you know I have children?"

"I know many things."

"Save us," Rhun grumbled tiredly. "Not *another* wise man. They afflict the earth these days as badly as would-be kings."

"I know of your children," Ynyr explained, "because of the way your eyes move when you speak of homes. I know of your children because of the way you stand and the way your lips and tongue curl round certain words and phrases. I know of them because of the inflection in your voice and the distant mistiness in your eyes when you say the word.

"I tell you that there is no future for them in a world controlled and ravaged by the Beast and his creatures. There is no safety for them, nowhere to hide, no future for them to look forward to. You say you have freedom? That is foolish talk indeed. You are slaves already, just as we are, for all that you may choose to ignore the chains that bind you. Time now for men of bravery to act. Time now to break those chains so that children may mature in ignorance of them."

"If the Slayers conquer all Krull," Colwyn added, seeing how Ynyr's words had shaken the bandit chief, "your children will be enslaved forever."

"Words." Torquil wrestled with an inner demon. "You twist words like a solicitor. How much is truth and how much built on this accursed fog, I cannot tell."

"What are we to do, Torquil?" asked an impatient, uncertain voice from behind a dead oak.

"Aye, the old man makes sense," said another.

"Shut up, you idiots, before the one who carries his sword as carefully as a swaddling babe learns each of your positions!" The woods went quiet.

But one of Torquil's band didn't wait for his chief's decision. The slim youth who stepped forward looked out of place alongside such experienced ruffians as Torquil and Sweyn. You had to look deeply into his eyes to see the pain and torment of an unhappy life, of events that had driven him into such company. Torquil frowned but said nothing.

"My name is Oswyn," the youth declared. "I am no chief and I have no children, but I do have a mind of my own." He glanced across at Torquil. "The old man speaks truth. I do think he uses his tongue not to twist words but to impart them. I have been a slave too long already." He looked up at Colwyn and lowered his voice.

"I will go with you. I have seen what the Slayers do to helpless villages and people. I would rather die fighting them with a sword in my hand."

"Thank you," said Colwyn gratefully. He looked off into the woods as he fingered his father's medallion, his eyes searching trees and rocks. "I need men to follow me. Men who are not afraid of Slayers or their own feelings. This boy is more man than any of you who hide behind selfish desires and trees. He shames you all."

The key he removed from the obverse of the medallion was

small but solid and very complex in design. He was taking a chance, he knew, in showing it to the desperate men who confronted him, but it seemed like a worthwhile risk. If they fought and he died here, they would likely discover it anyway. Neighboring kingdoms cooperated in such matters and this bog was not far from Turold. It seemed reasonable to assume that the key would work.

"Oswyn, give me your wrists." Uncertain but unafraid, the youth moved close. Colwyn slipped the key into the lock on the boy's right manacle and twisted. For a second nothing happened, but a little determined jiggling was rewarded by a gratifyingly loud *snap*. The manacle was rusty and full of grime. He repeated the action with the left band.

Oswyn backed away, rubbing his freed wrists and looking repeatedly from them to his benefactor. Colwyn sat back on his horse and tried to present a properly regal appearance. He was not very good at it and he kept one hand on the hilt of his sword.

The youth hesitated, still watching Colwyn, then bent and picked up the pair of opened manacles. He turned and wordlessly heaved them as far into the fog as he could. A distant splash told where they fell. When he turned back to Colwyn again, he was smiling.

Torquil had watched closely. Now he frowned thoughtfully up at Colwyn from beneath heavy brows, still not quite willing to countenance what his own eyes had just seen.

V

After a long moment he finally murmured carefully, "Only a king or a lord marshal would have keys to manacles like these, and you don't look much like a lord marshal. You're giving it a good try up on that fine horse, but somehow it doesn't suit you."

Colwyn relaxed in the saddle and grinned. "No, I guess it doesn't. You're right, fellow. I'm no lord marshal."

Torquil rubbed at his whiskers. "Matter of fact, what you do look like is about the right age to be the son of a certain king."

"Anything's possible," Colwyn admitted.

"King Turold's son, to be more precise."

"The exact age, in fact."

Torquil sighed and shook his head ruefully. "Ah, Torquil," he mumbled to himself, "it must be that you are growing old. Your brain is softening."

"But not your sword arm or your wits, I'd wager," Colwyn replied.

"I've no love for the kingdom of Turold. Its jails are neither better nor worse than those of any other country," the bandit growled. "Yet I must admit to having spent good times in its towns."

"There will be no more good times in any towns because there will be no towns nor even kingdoms in a few years unless we do away with the Slayers and their master," Colwyn declared firmly.

"Aye, so you say. So many claim. I am not certain I believe that yet, but I believe the rest. King Turold's son is named Colwyn."

"That is my name."

"And you would have *us* in your service? We hardly have the look of a royal guard." Guffaws came from his companions.

"It is not looks I need," Colwyn told him somberly. "Join me and help me, and you will all have a full pardon and whatever else it is in my power to grant." He reached down with the key. To his surprise, Torquil waved him off.

"Nay. If we succeed, unlock them. Otherwise, I will die with them." He smiled. "These cursed wristlets have already turned more than one sword stroke. Unlike young Oswyn there, I've developed a certain affection for them." He jangled the broken chains, then reached up and accepted the key to pass it to the man standing on his right. "Kegan here feels differently than I do, however."

"That I do, Torquil," said the man, rushing to unlock the manacles. Other men emerged from concealment, eager to make use of the key. "I harbor no fond memories of my iron," he told the man on horseback.

"Colwyn will suffice, Kegan. There are no kings on this journey. Only fighters."

"Rather a fighter defending my back than a king any day," said Kegan. "No offense, m'lor—Colwyn."

Colwyn formed an immediate liking for the man and wondered what terrible circumstance had forced so pleasant a fellow to follow so grim a path. Perhaps he would find out, though such men tended to guard their pasts as zealously as they did their gold.

"Nine like you are worth an army," he said as he inspected each of them in turn. "Soldiers spend too much time on secure, peaceful walls, too much time dreaming away easy nights in comfortable barracks. Each day you do battle with life itself. Soldiers have time to forget what their profession is all about. Like anything else, it is a trade that must be practiced to be perfected."

"Practice we've had aplenty," Torquil told him. He turned to his men. "You heard him, you smelly lot. It's official. We are now an army." There sounded a loud squeal and he looked down at his ankles. The piglet was easily swept up in the vagabond's arms.

"Well, well, our dinner comes to join us tonight. A fortunate meeting indeed." The pig squealed louder and squirmed in Torquil's grasp.

Colwyn peered closely at the porcine prisoner. "Don't be too quick to set a place. I think that's Ergo the Magnificent."

"Looks more like roast pork to me, though a mite skimpy. I certainly wouldn't call it magnificent." He prodded one ham.

The pig twisted violently. Torquil let out an exaggerated sigh. "Ah well. Shame. He's your companion, and I've yet to eat a friend, or even a friend of a friend."

"Look on the ground nearby. You'll probably find a scrap of paper with a formula written on it."

Obediently, Torquil bent to scan the damp earth, still cradling the unhappy porker. Perhaps they would be lucky

and there would be no such paper. He was hungry. Ah, but
there it was. He picked it up and scanned the writing. The
words and symbols meant nothing to him, but in his grasp the
pig squirmed excitedly. He held it before the questing snout.

Then he was holding a white cloud that was part pig and
part unhappy traveler. The cloud disappeared with a sharp
pop and he found himself grasping a small man by the back
of his shirt.

"Put me down, you lout! I can still turn you into a pig!"

"Yes, your demonstration of your powers has been most
convincing," Torquil said wryly.

"With hot fudge sauce, Ergo?" Colwyn inquired. Ergo
eyed him sourly but said nothing as Torquil let him go. He
tried to straighten his shirt and dignity, both of which were
badly ruffled.

"You had better manners as a pig," Torquil told him, "and
it's plain to see you're still something of a ham." He looked
up at Colwyn. "Of what use to you in your quest is this
midget?"

"Now look here, you hirsute oaf, I—"

"Peace, Ergo," said Colwyn tiredly. "And you, Torquil.
Every man has his talents to contribute." Ergo accepted that
and managed to calm himself. "We will need all the help we
can muster. Now we must go, now that everyone has been
properly introduced." He chucked his reins and started off
down the path. Torquil and his men followed.

Only Ergo, still miffed, hung back, shouting after them.
"Ergo the Magnificent does not travel with thieves and
cutthroats! I am no companion of bandits and murderers! I do
not lie down to sleep alongside pickpockets and wife-beaters!"

The fog swirled in around him, already masking Colwyn's
party. Shapes began to form in the fog, unworthy of notice
when traveling with companions but suddenly sharp and
demanding now that he stood by himself.

One of the gray nebulosities blinked; a single, one-eyed blink. Ergo gaped at it but it did not vanish.

"Except when necessary," he muttered to himself as he scurried after the others with admirable speed.

Several days of uneventful travel brought them to a hillside overlooking a devastated valley. Once it had been a picture of villatic contentment. Now it was a panorama out of hell.

Smoke rose not from cook pots and comforting fireplaces but from half a dozen burning towns. The wails of the distraught and the screams of injured men and dying animals rose from the smoking vale. Colwyn was glad they were not close enough to see any more than they could from the hillside. Silently the men resumed their trek along the crest of the heavily wooded ridge.

"Why do they burn the villages?" Torquil asked grimly as he marched alongside Colwyn. His gaze kept returning to the ruined valley. "There's nothing to gain. They never carry off booty or even food."

"They do it to keep us down," Ynyr explained. "Men who must concern themselves with rebuilding homes and replanting crops have no time to think of other things, no time for philosophy or science, learning or art. They force a lowly existence upon Krull."

"But why?"

Ynyr gave a little shrug. "Their intent is clear if not their ultimate motives. Perhaps they find it amusing to torment us. Perhaps they have other reasons." Torquil felt the old man wasn't telling all he knew, but the thief did not know how to pry the information out of him.

"You say there's nothing to gain," Colwyn told him. "You're wrong. There's fear to gain. You don't have to burn every village to control all. Raze one to the ground and the neighboring dozen may acknowledge your rule. Burn one valley and you might control a kingdom. They acquire such fear with fire. They spend it to rule.''

''So do many human kings.''

''But not all.''

''No, not all.'' Torquil grinned. King or not, this Colwyn of Turold was a likable chap. With the right kind of upbringing he might even have made a proper thief. Torquil could bestow no higher praise on a friend.

Ergo had been listening closely to this conversation as he shuffled along behind the horses. His eyes had widened as the import of the conversation became clear.

''Is he a . . . a king?''

The tall ruffian striding along next to him, one Bardolph by name, nodded once. ''Colwyn of Turold, or so Torquil believes. Heir to the combined kingdom of Turold and Eirig.'' He shook his head in disbelief at the circumstances that had overtaken him. ''From fugitive to king's service in one morning. I never thought to see such a day. I must say it's nice to be able to walk about freely in the daylight once again.''

Ergo cared little for Bardolph's musings, full as he was now of his own fearful misgivings. ''Oh dear, oh my. Oh *no*. I threatened to turn him into a toad. He might have done anything. He might have ordered my head chopped off.''

Bardolph instantly assumed a somber mien. ''As a matter of fact, I seem to recall some conversation to that point, friend. Yes, I remember distinctly now. He and Torquil were chatting and he reflected upon that very business.''

''What—what did he say?''

''He did order it. Your head to be cut off, I mean. He told Torquil, who referred it to me. I'd just forgotten all about it until you reminded me. 'Bardolph,' he said, 'chop that little man's head off. He'll never miss it.' '' As he spoke he was sliding a very long, gold-plated dagger from his belt. Now he thumbed the shiny edge and eyed Ergo speculatively.

Ergo backed away from him. "Stay away from me, you bloodthirsty hooligan! King's orders or no king's orders, I can still turn you into a toad."

Bardolph took a step toward him, smiling and fingering the blade meaningfully. "Or a pig, perhaps? I've seen your work and thus am quaking in fear. Come, make yourself useful and compliant all together. Turn yourself back into a pig. It's been some time since I've enjoyed fresh bacon."

"I'm warning you, I—" He stopped, frowned, and began sniffing at the air.

"What is it?" Bardolph asked curiously.

"I'm not sure. The fragrance of heaven, maybe."

Bardolph favored him with a look of disgust and slid the dagger back into its scabbard. "Well, don't linger too long over it or you'll find yourself left behind." He increased his stride and moved up to talk with Kegan.

Ergo fell off to one side. Still sniffing, he angled into the bushes, shoving branches aside as he progressed. A bush heavily laden with dark, pungent blotches soon came into view.

"Gooseberries! Ripe ones," he added in a tone usually reserved for funerals. He plucked one, popped it into his mouth and chewed. An expression of pure bliss came over him. "Ah, the nectar of paradise. Providence has taken pity on me and has seen fit to compensate me for the travails of the past days." He began picking at the bush, shoving gooseberries into his carry-pouch and every available pocket.

So intent was he on his task that he paid no attention to the rustling in the bushes nearby. When the crunching of leaves and twigs underfoot became too loud to ignore, he turned just in time to see the black face of a Slayer staring down at him. A handful of gooseberries fell to the ground, forgotten.

The Slayer stepped out of the copse. Ergo looked around wildly, too terrified to cry out and certainly beyond attempting any incantations. Big as the Slayer was, it seemed certain to remain unaffected by any mumblings he might muster, even if he succeeded in finding his voice.

Bending over, he grabbed up a broken branch and brandished it in the Slayer's direction. Its hand dropped to the battle-ax tied to its waist.

The bush on Ergo's left moved. Reflexively, his gaze moved from the Slayer to the bush, to see an enormous cyclops step into the clearing. He was holding a tree-sized trident, or so it appeared to Ergo. All this was too much for an essentially gentle mind. Ergo's eyes rolled up and he fell unconscious to the earth.

The Slayer too had taken note of the cyclops's appearance, but its reaction was not what Ergo would have anticipated. It let out a violent hiss, then whirled and retreated, crashing madly through the bushes. The cyclops considered its departure for a moment, then moved forward to bend over Ergo's crumpled body. Fingers touched Ergo's forehead. Then the one-eyed giant turned and hurried off in pursuit of the fleeing Slayer.

Colwyn turned in his saddle to look back along the line of men. He spoke to Torquil. "My friend is lingering longer than usual."

"Perhaps he had business in the trees," said Torquil noncommittally. Bardolph overheard and moved closer.

"We were, uh, jesting with each other when he smelled something and went exploring. I told him not to fall behind."

Colwyn's gaze returned to the empty trail behind them. "He'd better not. I don't want to lose time waiting up for him."

They heard the scream then. It hung long in the air, making

the horses start, before finally fading to silence. Somewhere behind them a life had disappeared along with that scream.

Colwyn turned his horse. "Back, and quickly!" The others rushed after him.

There had been an evening of the most exquisite delights, Ergo recalled, spoiled only by the unexpected early arrival of the young lady's husband. This propitiated the most unfortunate defenestration of the reveler, who was saved from a early death only by the fortuitous passage at the critical moment of a hay wagon beneath the good lady's window.

His head now reminded him of that night, for it throbbed as strongly as if he'd struck the street instead of the wagon. It seemed that the outraged husband had followed him even this far, for someone was peering into his eyes. Or into his eye, rather, for surely one could not penetrate where two could see? Or were there two eyes, small and bright red and alive with malicious intent? He could not tell. It was very confusing.

"There he is!" a voice shouted in the distance. The eye or eyes vanished. He struggled to call out but only a disreputable gargle emerged from his strained throat. Footsteps sounded close by. Then he remembered and tried to sit up.

A hand braced his shaky back. "Easy there, Ergo." That was Colwyn, he thought. Colwyn's voice and his strong arm. He did not remark on the familiarity between king and commoner. Colwyn was an uncommon king.

"Are you all right?" another voice inquired. Torquil there, examining the supine body. "Doesn't seem to be any bleeding. No sign of a wound."

"Only to my mind," Ergo mumbled. "Horrible. It was horrible." He tried to point, but discovered that his fingers shook as he gestured with them. "A creature with no eyes over there, and over there another with only one eye, and the both of them preparing to decide who was to have the pleasure of cutting me up, I'll wager."

"A cyclops," Ynyr murmured, raising his head to search the nearby trees with suddenly interested eyes, "and a Slayer. And our poor Ergo caught in the middle."

"I can't vouch for the Slayer, for he had yet to draw his weapon, but the one-eye was aiming a spear right at me! I would have turned him into a rat if . . . if . . ."

"If what?" asked Torquil.

Ergo's gaze fell. "I, uh, seem to have forgotten the formula."

"Nothing to be ashamed of, Ergo," Colwyn said reassuringly. "To be surprised by two such formidable individuals would give even a king pause."

"That's true," said Ergo, feeling much relieved.

Ynyr continued to study the surrounding trees. "If the cyclops had been aiming at you, my magnificent little friend, you'd be dead now instead of offering us descriptions of your intimidating visitors."

"If not at me, then who?"

Ynyr spoke without turning. "He was aiming at the Slayer, for there is an ancient hatred between them. It was the Slayer whose death rattle we heard, then.

"It is said that long ago the cyclopes' ancestors lived on a world far from Krull, and that they possessed two eyes like other humans. Then they made a bargain with the Beasts who command the Slayers; they gave up an eye apiece in return for the power of precognition."

Torquil's brow furrowed and Ynyr patiently explained. "The power to see into the future. But they were cheated, for the only futures they were sensitized to . . . permitted to see . . . were the times of their own deaths. It is said that precognition is but a dream even to the Beasts, but that by a certain artifice they can sometimes instill such an ability in others not of their race, in particular the means to see the time of death forthcoming. This they cannot do for themselves. It may be that they therefore experimented upon the unfortunate cyclopes, hoping to learn that which would enable them to make use of this ability themselves.

"There are others who say all this is so much myth and superstition. Of one thing there is no doubt. The cyclops are sad, solitary creatures, and they hate the Slayers and their master worse than any normal man, for it is not meet that anyone should have forewarning of his day of death."

"Today would have been my day, then," murmured Ergo as he climbed to his feet, "if it hadn't been for him. And I thought he meant me harm. I am ashamed."

"No reason to be," said Ynyr. "Their appearance is fearsome and they rarely seek human companionship. It may be that this one is different."

"Not very different," said Torquil. "You'll notice he didn't hang around to greet us."

"I am sorry he did not," said Ergo sadly, "for I would like to give him my thanks and offer my apology for having suspected ill of him."

"It would not matter to him one way or the other," Ynyr explained. "The cyclopes react the same to thanks or imprecations. Each attends to his or her own wants and cares nothing of what normal men think of them. If he saved you intentionally, and it seems certain that he did, he had reasons of his own for doing so."

"Reasons most excellent," Ergo agreed. Having reassembled, the expedition headed back toward the trail, but not before Ergo had checked to make sure that the terrifying fracas had not cost him his supply of dearly won gooseberries. He'd suffered too much to abandon them now.

Colwyn was not pleased to find that the trail climbed above the wooded ridge. Once more he found himself traversing bare rock broken only by the occasional wind-dwarfed tree. He did not like open, cold places. An imaginative man might find his mind wandering among the boulders and ravines, unwillingly transforming them into malign lines and designs.

That sharp, dark jumble of serrated granite off to his left, for example, might well be the exterior of the Black Fortress. That was a barrier he would confront soon enough, and he drew no joy from the image. He preferred to think only of Lyssa and the few moments they'd shared. The forest reminded him of her. The naked stone did not.

Odd how so powerful an attachment could be formed on the basis of so brief an encounter, he mused. It was as if they had been man and wife for years instead of merely newlyweds-to-be. It had surprised him then and had seemed to surprise her as well. Only Ynyr did not seem surprised at the extent of Colwyn's feelings for a woman but fleetingly met. But then, little seemed to surprise Ynyr. Turold had been very different.

Thoughts of his father turned Colwyn's mood dark and he fought to concentrate on other things. Consider the side of the mountain they were approaching, for example. That was an object devoid of emotional overtones. Bare rock was no candidate for melancholy reflection. It was an elemental vision that brooked no mental coloration, a cliff of clean granite towering several thousand feet cloudward. There is no false pretense in stone, he thought. It can be trusted with idle thoughts.

He looked over toward Ynyr. The old man sat stolidly in his saddle, staring straight ahead. There was nothing in his posture or expression to indicate that he intended to change direction. Colwyn studied the cliff they were approaching more intently. It could not be climbed.

Ynyr finally stopped at the base of the mountainside and dismounted. Colwyn did the same. The old man spoke to the young king and to Torquil.

"We three will go."

"Go where?" The bandit chief eyed the cliff unhappily.

"Up that? I have strong fingers and have been in some difficult places, old man, but I am not a bird."

"Nor am I," Ynyr reminded him. "We are not going to do any climbing." He glanced past him. "The rest of you will remain here to guard the horses."

"We *four* will go." Ergo hastened to join them. "I'm not staying here with these criminals!"

"Why, what's wrong, Ergo?" asked Kegan. "Don't you trust us?" Behind him, a grinning Bardolph lightly fingered the point of his golden dagger.

"It's not that," Ergo answered, hastening to soothe any injured feelings. "Only that I could not think of allowing my Lord Colwyn to place himself in danger where I could not be of assistance to him."

"Aye, I see your point," said Kegan. "One never knows when one might encounter a band of Slayers who could be terrified into submission by the sight of a hysterical pig." The other escapees joined in his laughter.

With great dignity Ergo turned and followed the others. "It is also clear that my advice is not appreciated by those of lower intelligence." This last was whispered aloud only when he was well out of sword reach.

Colwyn sighed indulgently. "Very well. We *four* will go." He looked to Ynyr.

"As you wish. It will not matter once we are inside."

Ergo didn't like the sound of that but saw no way of backing down. He was committed to whatever lay *inside*. Out of the tart into the pie pan, he thought. Better the other way around. Oh well, glory awaits. But he took care to stay well behind Colwyn and Ynyr. There was no point in rushing on to glory.

A modest hike brought them to an open place before a sheer cliff. Ergo took a moment to try ingratiating himself further with the leader of the escaped prisoners.

"He marches us straight toward the sheer face of the rock." He nodded at Ynyr. "The old man has raisins in his braincase."

"And you have fruit on the brain," Torquil replied. "You and I should have such raisins." He stopped and put out a restraining arm, which knocked the breath from the smaller man. "Hold. See? Some magic is about to happen."

Ergo stared. Ynyr stood at the foot of the cliff, waiting patiently and doing nothing. "What magic? He stands like one paralyzed. That is not magic. Constipation, perhaps, but not magic."

Torquil glared at him. "You have no respect for your elders."

"I never got anything from my elders except beatings and bad advice." He gestured at the motionless Ynyr. "Why should I look differently on this one?"

As he spoke, the face of the cliff began to change. Sheets of flowing green appeared, a bright wash of color that covered a portion of the bare rock. Ynyr stepped forward . . . to be swallowed up by the waterfall as though the stone beyond had vanished. Colwyn followed. Torquil glanced meaningfully down at his companion.

Ergo shrugged. "All right, so that's a good reason. I didn't see *him* do anything, though." But the condition of his belly belied his words as he watched the disdainful Torquil disappear into the green cascade.

First you threaten to turn a king into a toad and now you dispute a true wise man's knowledge. It was a wonder he was still alive.

For several moments he debated whether to follow or return to the camp. As he hesitated, he fingered the interior of a pocket. He was already out of gooseberries. Nothing to live for, then.

Cursing under his breath at having fallen in with such a

group of visionaries and thieves, he reluctantly hurried to catch up with the others.

"Mad," he mumbled as he stepped anxiously into the waterfall. "They're all mad."

VI

Inside they found themselves walking down a passageway lit by the same cool green glow that had suffused the waterfall. It led inward and down. The slope was gentle.

Colwyn was glad of the coolness. He'd recently found himself inside a mountain cave where the air was considerably less hospitable. Clearly this place was nothing like the cavern of the glaive. There was no steam, no sign of lava or stink of sulfur. The temperature stayed pleasant as they walked, though he wondered at the complete absence of any breeze.

The tunnel made a sharp turn to the right and opened onto a spacious chamber that had been hollowed from the rock by some unknown force. Light penetrated from above, so bright that its source could not be discerned. The walls and ceiling were smooth and relatively featureless. Colwyn could not tell if the chamber had been formed by natural forces or the hand of man.

The room was sparsely decorated. A few draperies and hangings, utensils and plates of common shape and manufacture. On a simple seat sat an old man whose gaze seemed to be elsewhere. Colwyn advanced, his eyes never leaving the white-bearded figure. He noted the way the eyes twitched absently, never focusing on anything in particular.

Seer or not, this old man would seek his visions without the aid of normal sight. He was quite blind. Close by sat a young boy whose eyes never left the visitors. The child's movements were short and quick. Colwyn thought of the cats that infested Turold Castle. Here in this boy they surely had a quiet, two-legged relation.

The stone that rested before the old man elicited a gasp of admiration from Torquil, professional reliever of other men's possessions that he was. The emerald glowed with a powerful inner light and was no less than the size of the old man's head. Colwyn suspected that it was not the ordinary stone of Torquil's avaricious dreaming but rather a colorful manifestation of much more, just as its owner's vision extended into realms other men saw only as darkness and mystery.

The old man's hands moved through a picture hovering above the pulsating gem: the image of four wanderers. Colwyn had no difficulty recognizing his companions and himself. The wrinkled fingers swept easily through the image like birds through a cloud, without altering or distorting it. Unable to sense their presence with his eyes, the seer was tasting of his visitor's essence via means they could not fathom.

"I recognize an old friend," he said softly. Ynyr motioned for Colwyn and the others to wait. He stepped forward toward the seer. The boy watched carefully.

"A fellow student of knowledge," the seer continued, his fingers picking at smoke.

Ergo and Torquil did not have to be ordered to stay back. Such activities gave the prosaic thief the shivers, while Ergo finally allowed himself to relax. Torquil moved off by himself, intent on the bright crystals that poked from the rocks.

A voice drew Ergo's attention. "My name is Titch." The boy had come up quietly alongside him. He offered milk in a cup. Ergo accepted with thanks, though wishing for something stronger as he watched the two wise men.

"Greetings, friend of my youth," said Ynyr. "I see that your seeing is little changed."

The seer's smile widened slightly. "Alas, I see that which others cannot see, and would gladly trade all for the ability to see as they do. Such is not my fate, however. How may I assist you?"

Ynyr took a deep breath. Friend or not, the seer still abided by certain rules and restrictions. Would he aid them, even if he could?

"We seek the Black Fortress."

The seer nodded as if acknowledging something beyond their ken. "I suspected it was no simple request that brought you this far. Such a vision will be opposed. This is not the kind of request I expected from you, old friend. The Black Fortress, you say. Who seeks it?"

"The new king."

"King of what?"

"Of Turold and Eirig and perhaps a greater realm still . . . if fortune travels with us."

"A capricious traveling companion indeed. As for this new king you speak of, I know him not."

Colwyn stepped forward to stand next to Ynyr. "I am here, espier of the distant mysteries. Ynyr serves me and my purpose."

"Ynyr serves no man, be he king or commoner," said the seer with a knowing smile that made Colwyn wonder, "but while your reasons may differ, I see that your purposes are the same." Colwyn did not comment. Let the seer believe what he wished. All Colwyn wanted was the way to Lyssa.

"He does not speak," said the seer.

"For a young man he is wise," Ynyr said.

"Very well then. I will seek the Fortress for you." He pushed back his sleeves and leaned forward to press both hands tight against the emerald . . . if emerald it was. Torquil was no longer so certain. There was a hint of something else about the stone. Could it be another substance made to look like an emerald? A roundabout way to hide a secret.

As he stared, the irregular green object began to spin on its axis. A deep whir emerged from green depths. It reminded Torquil of a waterwheel at flood time. Soon it was rotating rapidly enough to make him dizzy and he found he had to turn his gaze away from it.

A shape was close at his side and he had to force himself not to jump. Damn, but the boy could move quietly!

Titch held the stoneware pitcher. Irritated at his nervousness, Torquil declined a refill. The boy turned to Ergo, repeated the offering.

"Milk gives me gas. Can't handle too much of the stuff," Ergo explained. "Got any sugar balls?"

"No."

"Gumdrops? Caramel ladies? Chocolate strings or honey-dew squares?"

"No, sir," said Titch apologetically.

Ergo looked displeased. "What kind of boy are you? Boys always have candy. Though perhaps I am asking too much. This is no normal home for a child. I should not be surprised that you have no access to sweets."

The boy thought a moment, then brightened, eager to please. He fumbled in a pocket. "I have a cinnamon bar."

"Ah, sweets in a sour place after all." A beatific smile

spread over Ergo's face. Titch held the bar out to his guest but Ergo shook his head.

"Your hospitality is admirable for one so young, but I will not take all your candy. Share and share alike's my motto." Having said this, he extended a hand.

Titch grinned and broke the bar in two. Ergo's graciousness did not prevent him from taking the larger half and popping it into his mouth.

"Thank you, boy. My stomach was growing tired of naught but healthful food. For that boon I will tell you my full name. I am"—he hesitated, chewing and trying not to mumble the words—"Ergo the Magnificent. Short in stature, tall in power, narrow of purpose, wide of vision." He looked at the boy. "What do you think of that, eh?"

"That is very impressive, sir," Titch admitted.

"I should hope so." Ergo smiled contentedly as he masticated the spicy remnants of the cinnamon bar.

The boy glanced away, embarrassed. "I am Titch."

"So you said. Not impressive, but adequate." The boy looked pleased and Ergo beamed at him. He was thoroughly enjoying his favorite role—that of the powerful but benign dispenser of small favors.

Being somewhat less than interested in this wordplay, Torquil had moved off to one side. He'd set his cup on the floor and checked to make certain no one was watching him. Now was the time to check out something that had intrigued him since they'd first entered the seer's cave.

He still was not certain of the composition of the massive green object that spun in the air before the seer, but as to the nature of many similar small shapes lining the walls he was more confident. He pried at them with his knife and was gratified to find that they came free of their binding matrix with ease. Ignoring the magic the old men played at, he pleasured himself by filling his pockets with the long, vitreous emerald crystals.

Now the seer seemed to be staring intensely at nothingness. The great emerald was a wild blur in the center of the chamber, its outlines no longer distinct, its substance malleable. Sparks shot between the old man's fingers and the rotating mass. Colwyn watched in awe and thought of small lightning. His vocabulary did not contain the words necessary to describe what he was seeing, but he was certain of one thing: there was great power at work here, ancient power, power of the sort Ynyr had casually alluded to during their journey. Power enough, perhaps, to surprise even the Beast at rest in his Fortress.

An image began to form above the explosively rotating green mass, changing and contorting as it began to coalesce, gathering strength and outline. Colwyn watched as walls and towers of alien design began to take shape. They had not been designed by human hands to please human eyes. They were constructed of the maybe-stone that teased the senses.

As the seer leaned toward the emerald blur, it seemed certain that the lightning must consume his hands. Suddenly an inhuman scream of rage erupted from within the green. A black claw emerged from nowhere to shatter emerald and image alike. It followed both into oblivion.

The violence of the confrontation had sent the seer tumbling backward. Fragments of green-tinged electricity hung for long seconds in the air. Colwyn ignored the sharp fragments of green that had gone flying as he rushed to help the old man.

"Are you hurt?"

"No." The seer reached up and accepted the leverage of Colwyn's arm. His smile was grim. "Am I cut or otherwise injured where I cannot see?"

Colwyn looked him over. "No. By some miracle the

splinters missed us all." Ynyr's smile told him that the fact they had not been cut to ribbons had nothing to do with any imagined miracle.

The seer dusted himself off as he spoke. "The Beast does not like curious humans poking into his private affairs. This in itself is a challenge to his mortality and the veil of omnipotence he chooses to wear. I was not quite able to pinpoint the location of the Fortress, I am sorry to say, but at least we have managed to upset his day. That alone was worth the intervention."

"His power is too great for you to overcome?" Ynyr asked.

"Yes. Here." The seer gestured toward the center of the chamber and the remnants of the emerald mass. "This was but a poor device, incapable of sharp focus over a long distance. There is better, and it reposes in a place where his power cannot reach, where old shields still function."

"The Emerald Temple," Ynyr murmured, nodding knowingly. "I was told when still young that it had been reduced to the status of a myth."

"No. It exists still, the best protected relic of our golden age, my friend. In that place he cannot oppose my vision."

"By going there we risk exposing its location to him."

"I think it worth the risk," the seer replied, "if this young man is truly the one king you speak of."

"He is that," said Ynyr, "and more. We go to rescue his bride-to-be."

"Ah, that would be the Lady Lyssa. Yes, that is worth the risk."

Colwyn listened carefully to this elderly dialogue. There was much hidden meaning here, if only one possessed the wits to unlock the secrets these old men discussed. Alas, real knowledge lay buried beneath a flurry of half-truths and partial revelations.

"Will you travel there with us, then?" Ynyr inquired.

"It lies deep within the Wyn-nah-Mabrug, the Great Swamp, where the earth itself consumes unlucky travelers. It is a long time since I trod the way."

"Our need is great. You have already acknowledged that it is worth the risk," Colwyn said, pressing for a decision.

"No need to fret, my young king." The seer rose from his seat. "Having agreed with your purpose, I must fit my own feelings to your needs. Of course I will accompany you." He turned. "Titch, prepare my things." The boy nodded and disappeared into a side tunnel. The seer listened to his haste and smiled.

"A quiet boy, an orphan I took in when no others would. He is fleet of foot and mind and has the sense to listen when most his age do naught but chatter incessantly. He has been useful to me. In return, I care for his needs and do my poor best to educate him." He turned away from his guests, murmuring softly. "Education escapes those who are not of a mind to listen. Such see only what they wish to see."

Torquil nodded dutifully at this wisdom while making certain his recent crystalline acquisitions remained hidden behind his back.

Bare mountainsides and dead woods, cloying fog and valleys aflame, and now this, Colwyn mused as they approached the edge of the Wyn-nah-Mabrug. Surely somewhere on Krull there was a land of soft green hills and clear skies, where the people went about their daily tasks contentedly and tragedy did not mar their every thought. He longed for such a sanctuary even as he knew such restfulness was not for him. Not while Lyssa remained a prisoner and bands of Slayers roamed the land with impunity. Someone had to do something. He had not chosen this path. It had chosen him.

He was more right than he knew.

The seer raised a hand for the party to halt. "We must

dismount here, at the edge of the Great Swamp. The ground is too treacherous to support the weight of horses.''

Hands helped him down, moved to assist the somber Titch. As the horses were being tethered, a brooding Kegan walked over to whisper to Torquil.

"We went to a lot of trouble to get those horses. Ten to one they won't be here when we get out of that.'' He nodded sharply toward the swamp ahead. "*If* we get out.''

"Come now, my friend,'' Torquil murmured softly, "do you think old Torquil would lead you on a journey without profit? Don't worry about the horses. We can buy more if necessary.''

"There has been much talk of driving off the Slayers and of saving the land, of destinies and duties. I agreed to come along with that 'king' because it seemed meet to do so at the time, and because you made the decision. But in my heart I long for a visit to some city where we may again lighten the purses of those fat citizens who would keep our faces in the dirt.''

"Those days will come again, my friend, if we lose our promised pardon. Meanwhile take heart. All is not as bleak as it may appear.''

"Is it not?'' Kegan let out a derisive snort. "So far all I see are losses and the potential of more.''

Torquil slipped a hand into one back pocket and felt of the slim, cool shapes lying there. "Patience, Kegan, patience.''

The other thief noted Torquil's tone as well as the movement of his hand. "Now, what secret would you be toying with there, good Torquil?''

"Not one to reveal here and now,'' came the reply. He nodded over to where Colwyn was in discussion with the two wise men. "There are eyes here that might frown on a little harmless work.'' With that he moved away, leaving a frustrated but intrigued Kegan to wonder what his chief was talking about.

"Ah, my friends," Torquil said pleasantly as he approached the triumvirate, "how are we to proceed? The day will not wait on us and I'd as soon spend as few nights as possible in such a place."

The seer raised a hand and pointed into the morass. "The temple lies near the center of the swamp, which comes very near dry land here. The place we seek is marked by three trees that grow as one." He reached out and placed a hand on Titch's shoulders. "Many's the time I've instructed the boy on its location, so it should not be lost should anything happen to me. He knows the way as well as I."

"You ask us to follow the lead of a blind man and a boy," Torquil muttered to Colwyn. "You ask much."

"I promise much. In any case we have no choice, my friend. This is no time for hesitation." He nodded toward the swamp. "'Tis a wonder that even bog plants can grow in such a place. It smells of death."

"Power and death are cousins," Ynyr offered. "They have much in common."

"Not to me they don't." Torquil found the analogy displeasing. "I don't much like your relatives, old man."

"As the gentleman has pointed out," the seer murmured, "we waste the daylight." Steadying himself with Titch he started confidently forward into the swamp. Muck sucked at his boots and leggings but did not drag him down. Colwyn and Ynyr followed while Ergo boldly preceded the disgruntled but resigned thieves.

At least it wasn't raining, Colwyn thought. They were not as miserable as they might have been. He recalled the last time they'd traversed such a place and wondered if similar thoughts had occurred to Torquil. If so, they did not show on the bandit chief's face. Colwyn lengthened his stride until he was walking alongside the boy. Titch watched the ground carefully, leading the seer by the hand.

"Is this the only route?"

Titch nodded. "The only one I was taught, sir."

"There is only the one way," the seer added. "If we deviate from it even slightly, we will find ourselves swallowed by the quicksands that abound here. What troubles you about our path?"

"I dislike traveling any terrain where the air itself gives cover to potential assailants." He nodded toward the lake off to their left. "Follow the shoreline as closely as possible, boy. That way we'll only have to watch one side."

"I will try to do so, sir."

"Awkward country." Colwyn unconsciously fingered the hilt of his sword. "Not even a safe line of retreat. Keep a sharp lookout. If we can penetrate this swamp, so can our enemies."

"The same thought had already occurred to me. I have already warned the others to be on the alert," said Torquil.

Colwyn clapped him on the back and moved down the line to chat with the rest of his men, reassuring himself even as he reassured them.

Ergo slipped an errant gooseberry, one of several he had acquired earlier, from one pocket and popped it quickly into his mouth . . . but not quite quickly enough.

"I smell gooseberries," said Titch excitedly. He hesitated, sniffing the moist air, then glanced wide-eyed at Ergo.

"Ah well, share and share alike. It seems I've found some I'd forgotten, just in time to part with them. Your nose is as big as your eyes, boy."

"The seer says that a man should not be guided by any one sense but should learn to utilize all at his command. He says that in this way we may better master our surroundings."

"Even to including gooseberries, it would seem." Ergo

fished through one voluminous pocket, brought out one last handful, and passed them to the boy.

"Thank you, magnificence!"

His master has taught him courtesy, Ergo mused. Not to mention the ability to estimate the stature of those around him.

"Don't mention it."

The boy was downing them one at a time, luxuriating over the flavor and texture of each individual berry. "Truly you are a wizard fit to consort with my master. Only one of true ability could conjure up treats like this."

Yes, most courteous and perceptive, Ergo decided as he fumbled through another pocket. "Here, boy," he said magnanimously, "have a few more. Now, tell me that about my ability again?"

Torquil kept silent until Colwyn had concluded his inspection and returned to the forefront of the troupe. Then the bandit leader slowed his walk until he fell in next to Kegan. He reached into a pocket, withdrew a small cloth pouch.

"If you want to see the profit of this journey, take a look in this."

Kegan eyed him uncertainly for a moment, then took the pouch. He extracted a handful of rocks. Dull, gray, featureless pebbles. Crystals of sand and mica and feldspar. He stared intently at them, thinking he might be missing something, before returning his gaze to his chief.

"They're worth a fortune," Torquil was whispering, his gaze still on Colwyn. "And I memorized the location well. Plenty of time after we finish with this business to return and gather up all we can carry. The smallest alone's worth a king's ransom."

"Maybe," replied Kegan dryly, "to someone who's very nearsighted, or heir to a very poor kingdom."

"What? What are you blathering . . . ?" He gaped at Kegan's open palm. "Where did you get those rocks?"

"From your pouch full of profit."

"That's not possible! I took only the finest—" He broke off as he dug into his other pockets, pulling out handfuls of narrow gray stones. No green light burned in their depths, no promise of the easy life shone from glassy surfaces. Numb, he let them fall to the ground. The only light they threw back at him came from bits of quartz embedded in the matrix.

Kegan was shaking his head, his voice pitying. "Poor Torquil, once the finest thief on the north continent, now reduced to this. Remind me to steal you some reading glasses."

Torquil tore his gaze from the place where he'd dropped the worthless rocks and all but snarled at his companion. "I swear to you, they were emeralds. Emeralds the size of a man's hand!"

"The size of a man's dreams, maybe." Kegan strode out in front, still shaking his head.

"Perhaps the wealth was in your heart and not in the stones."

Torquil looked around sharply. "What? Who said that?" He tried to see who'd spoken but could not. The seer was too far ahead for the bandit to notice the old man's faint smile.

The lake on their left seemed as big as the swamp itself, and Colwyn was grateful for the way it shielded their exposed flank. They were able to concentrate ahead and to their right. All save Torquil, that is. He spent his time staring at the ground and muttering to himself, his brow occasionally twisting with the strain of confused thoughts.

Only one member of the party really let his eyes wander: Ergo the Magnificent. After all, it was hardly his place to participate in the work of professional cutthroats, especially if one were inclined to more culturally elevating pursuits such as inspecting passing bushes for their gooseberry content.

Irony has a way of bestowing responsibilities, however, and it was his roving gaze that happened to fix on the supposedly secure left flank, just as clawed, alien shapes began silently rising from the water, dripping green scum and camouflaging moss. If not for Ergo's wandering eye, the surprise might have been total.

As it was, his fright was strong enough to stifle the first cries of alarm in his throat. It took his vocal cords another precious minute to engage.

"SLAYERS!"

The little procession whirled. Colwyn spotted the emerging assailants first. "There, from the lake! Torquil, get the wise men to safety!" Sword drawn and ready, the bandit leader hurried to comply.

"Oswyn, Darro, you heard the king!" The two men rushed to escort the elderly noncombatants out of range while the rest engaged the Slayers.

Even as the seer and Ynyr were being hustled back down the trail, other Slayers were materializing to block any retreat. A single spear transfixed the unfortunate Darro, who never saw his killer. A bolt of energy sped straight at Titch. Moving like the whirlwind he occasionally became, Ergo leaped forward and knocked the boy to the ground. Later he would swear that the bolt cursed as it exploded over their heads.

The pair of Slayers pressed Oswyn hard as they attempted to reach the seer, but he kept them off until help arrived in the form of Colwyn and Torquil. The Slayers were large and powerful, but slow to react. In combat with men they relied for success on numbers and their strange energy weapons. In close quarters the two were no match for the tough escapees.

No one saw a third Slayer rise slowly from the bog on the opposite side of the trail to aim his spear at Ynyr's back. The blast of energy never reached its intended target. It fell from the hand that had gripped it as a trident of peculiar design pierced the Slayer's neck.

Other Slayers continued to rise from the lake, but with the element of surprise now fled, they were evenly matched against Torquil's band. Men fighting for freedom always fight harder than those fighting as slaves, and now they confirmed Colwyn's decision to enlist them in his cause.

Soon the murky surface of the lake was clean once more and the air smelled of destroyed Slayers. Colwyn walked over to join Torquil, who was cleaning his muddy ax on a legging.

"How many did we lose? I was too busy to see."

"Only Darro."

Colwyn turned to the now quiescent lake. "I'm sorry. I knew him but briefly. He struck me as a good man unjustly wronged."

"A very good man." Torquil's tone was somber. "Made a pariah and an outlaw for daring to love the daughter of a powerful nobleman."

"Did she love him back?"

"So Darro always insisted, no matter how hard we teased him about it."

"Then surely there was no crime in it," Colwyn said. "When this is over I will make certain that his name is expunged from any criminal records where it appears, and that his family is told in whose service and how well he sold his life."

"Darro would've liked that. Few men choose crime for a profession. It always seems to choose them."

"I know how the fates can set one on a path he never imagined, nor even wishes for himself. What of you, friend Torquil? What troubles placed you on this sorry path?"

"Another time, Colwyn, mayhap I'll tell you." He gestured up the trail. "For the moment, it seems we have lost one man only to find another to take his place."

Colwyn followed his pointing finger. "One, I see, who may be worth more than any three, though 'tis no man who stands before us."

They approached the newcomer. His recovered trident in hand, the cyclops stood between Ergo and Titch, towering over them. His single eye regarded them benignly.

Ergo was forced to lean back in order to see the disconcerting face of their rescuer. "This is the second time you've saved my life. I admit to feeling some apprehension the first time our paths crossed."

"That is quite understandable." There was nothing but gentleness in the cyclops's voice. "My appearance is upsetting to most men, something which I regret but refuse to apologize for, as I am not responsible for it."

"I am Ergo." He extended a welcoming hand, saw it vanish in the vast but easy grip.

"The Magnificent, if I am not mistaken?"

Ergo tried to hide his annoyance. "He appears to have compensated for the loss of an eye by developing a talent for eavesdropping," he muttered to Titch. "Doesn't he have a name? But why do I ask you? So terrifying a vision would obviously send a child such as yourself fleeing in terror at its mere sight."

"Not really," said Titch apologetically. "His name is Rell. I've met him before." The cyclops smiled down at the boy. "He visits the seer sometimes. He doesn't talk much and when he and my master converse they use words that are beyond me. He lets my master do most of the talking. I don't think he likes to talk."

"So I've noticed. Except to be sarcastic to those who wish to be friends."

"Or to talk with those who already are friends," the cyclops commented.

Ergo was still reluctant to forgive the slight. "My name is not for jesting with, beanpole. It's all very well and good to have a short name when you're twelve feet tall, but small people need large names to give them weight."

"Your actions give you more weight than any name could, my sensitive friend," the giant told him somberly. "I saw you save the boy from the spear. That was worth a hundred noble titles. I've seen many *noble* men turn tail and flee when confronted with such a choice. He who takes the risk to save another honors his name in deed far more than can be done by any combination of letters."

Embarrassment was a posture Ergo rarely suffered from, but it made him turn away now. "Well, there's no need to make a fuss over it. It was easy. No spear was coming at me. Besides, it's what friends are supposed to do for one another."

"Exactly so," said the cyclops. "Don't try to shrug it off. Your heroism is much more real than your affected magnificence."

"What do you mean 'affected'?" Ergo demanded to know, back on emotionally comfortable ground again.

The cyclops sighed. "Never have I met a man so intent on avoiding a well-deserved compliment. Do not think to avoid it so easily, my friend. What I *can* see, I see clearly and without distortion."

Colwyn arrived in time to cut off Ergo's ready rejoinder.

"Ah," said the cyclops, "so this is the man who claims to be king of more than a kingdom." He studied the new arrival carefully. "What's wrong, man? Are you not content with one kingdom that you must lay claim to more?"

"I did not choose this course of action, one-eye. It was thrust upon me by circumstance."

"Ah, circumstance," the cyclops mused aloud. "I could tell you much about circumstance, young king."

"I hope that I may have the opportunity to listen," Colwyn nodded toward Ergo. "You've been paralleling our course for some time now. Shadowing our companion here."

Ergo puffed up like a toad-frog. "It's only natural he would be attracted to an obviously superior type."

"Not to mention one with a propensity for wandering off on his own and drawing the attention of marauding Slayers," Colwyn reminded him.

"It's true I have been following you," the cyclops admitted. "I would still be keeping my own company if not for the need to aid His Magnificence on several occasions." Both waited for a response from Ergo but that worthy wisely elected to hold his peace this time.

The cyclops nodded across to where Ynyr was conversing softly with the seer. "When I learned that the old one had come down off his mountain I knew that the time had come."

"Time for what?" Colwyn asked curiously.

"The time for decision-making. It's something the seer and I talked of on many occasions. Being wise, he was not intimidated by my size and since he is blind, I was not intimidated by his knowledge. We got along well."

"I can see why, for though your appearance may be fearsome to many, I find your openness and perceptivity appealing. There is no need to keep to the bush and rocks. Travel *with* us, instead of alongside us. All men need company."

The cyclops smiled broadly. "Yes. All men. I think that you will make a good king, Colwyn. If you live." He turned and walked off to inspect the lakeshore.

Colwyn beckoned to Torquil. "What do you think of our new ally?"

"He's agreed to join us, then?"

"It seems he'd already done so, though for reasons of his

own he chose not to announce it until now. I've invited him to share our company as well as our purpose.''

Torquil looked to where the cyclops was probing the water with his huge trident. ''I'm glad you did so. He'll be a fit replacement for poor Darro, and in any fight he'll be worth half a dozen men. His kind hates the Slayers, and if there are any spoils to be taken he'll not demand a share. A better fighting companion would be hard to imagine.''

''I'm glad you approve.'' Colwyn watched the cyclops at his work. ''Though I'm not sure your opinion of him matters any more than does mine.''

''How do you mean?''

''He'd already decided he was going to join us. Come. Let's get out of this place and hope there are no more ambushes waiting for us. I'm as anxious as any man to breathe clean air again.''

VII

Though she ran down endless corridors, she had no way of marking the passage of time. She did not grow hungry, and nervousness alone kept her from collapsing from fatigue. That, and a determination to run until she was stopped.

She wished for the rats that would normally infest such a place, but this was no ordinary fortress. Even common vermin shunned its peculiar tunnels and passages.

Then the gown and robe appeared before her again, its glowing crown a floating promise of an awful, unimaginable destiny.

"Why have I been brought here?" she asked.

And she heard the voice of the Beast, not as an echoing roar that filled the corridors, but as words, carried to her in a tone of sly confidence.

"For a ceremony."

"What kind of ceremony?"

"Do you not recognize before you a gown such as no

woman has ever seen or dreamed of? Do you not recognize the crown that can only be worn by a queen wedded to He Who Commands? You have been brought here for a wedding.''

She was too frightened to scream. She turned to retreat back the way she'd come, but a white Slayer stood there, impassively threatening. With a weak cry she turned and stumbled off still deeper into the maze. . . .

It was strange to find such an extensive strip of dry land in the middle of the Great Swamp, but the narrow bridge of earth and gravel was a welcome sight to the marchers. They'd been straining their eyes on the faint path ever since they'd entered the Great Swamp lest they step out on a surface that might suddenly disappear. It was a relief to stride, however briefly, on land that did not swallow a man's ankles.

Titch had fallen back, leaving the uncomplaining seer to walk with Ergo to guide him. The boy was drawn to the cyclops. Now he rode atop the giant's shoulders. In addition to being fun, it provided him with the best vantage point of all.

''That way,'' he would announce from time to time, and the group would obediently alter direction to comply with his directions.

''What's it like being able to see out of only one eye?'' he asked innocently.

''Never having had the pleasure of looking at the world out of two, I cannot say for sure,'' the cyclops replied thoughtfully, ''but from my occasional conversations with two-eyed men, I gather it's something like squinting all the time. I cannot see as widely, but what I do see I see with great clarity. Close one eye of your own and you will see what I mean.''

The boy complied. ''That's not so bad.''

"There are worse infirmities a man can suffer. Better one eye lost than an arm or leg."

"If it was in my power to do so I'd give you the other one back," Titch told him solemnly.

"I know you would, boy. My people made a bad bargain with the Slayers' master. Perhaps someday we will have a chance to start anew. I will not see that day, but I can hope that it comes to children born of one-eyed mothers."

Ergo waited until the conversation lagged before commenting. "If I had *my* wish I'd be out of this miserable place right now. And if I really had a wish I'd be sitting on top of a gooseberry trifle the size of a mountain."

"Greed has been the cause of death in many a man," observed Ynyr. He spoke to Ergo but his gaze was on Torquil. Or was it? These damned wise men, the bandit grumbled to himself. You never can tell what they're thinking about you. Always they talk in riddles in order to keep us poor common folk bemused as to their real intentions. It would be better if they were easily understood.

Of course, that would make whoever understood them a wise man himself. Torquil pondered this as they marched deeper into the Wyn-nah-Mabrug.

"Perhaps you're right, old man," Ergo replied. "Maybe I am too greedy. I am willing to scale down my desires, yea, even my wishes. So I'd settle for a trifle as big as a house." Ynyr made a disgusted face and said no more. Clearly this Ergo was beyond learning wisdom.

Titch's face had been wrapped in deep thought while the adults talked. Now he brightened. "I'd wish for a puppy."

"A typical child's thought. I'd have thought better of you, boy," Ergo said. "Why not wish for gold, or power? That way you could buy or command all the puppies you desired."

Titch shook his head, his voice soft. "One puppy would be enough for me."

"Just one? As long as you're wishing why not make full use of your wish? Why not wish for a hundred?"

Titch shook his head stubbornly. "What would I do with a hundred puppies?"

"Sell ninety-nine of them."

"A man after my own heart," murmured Torquil, but somehow it did not fill the air with the freshness of a compliment. Ergo decided to ignore it.

"I only want one," Titch repeated, so sadly that Ergo decided not to trouble the boy further. Instead he lowered his attention and questions out.

"A foolish wish. And you, Rell. What would you wish for? A one-eyed beauty to make your mate? A trident of pure gold? Or perhaps a small kingdom of your own?"

The single eye managed to match Ergo's two. "Ignorance."

Ergo was ready with a reply, hesitated, thought better of it, and subsided. They walked on in silence.

It seemed that the mist had dispersed a little when they made the sharp turn to the right. Afterward no one could say exactly what happened. The ground sank from under their feet without any warning.

One moment all were striding confidently along and the next, half the party found themselves struggling in thick soup that clutched powerfully at their legs.

"Quicksand!" Kegan roared even as he threw himself backward and searched for a solidly anchored handhold.

Those who remained on firm ground rushed to aid the trapped. Even Ynyr lent a hand, though the seer could only stand out of the way and give moral support. Ergo, Titch and Ynyr linked hands, the old man clinging to a gnarled tree trunk, Ergo reaching out over the muck to extend a hand to Oswyn. They soon had him extricated.

Bardolph was caught close to several low-hanging trees and Torquil was able to pull him free without help. The thief slid

clear of the danger easily. He was breathing hard as he stood
and felt of himself. Suddenly his eyes dropped to his waist
and then glanced sharply toward the false trail that had nearly
claimed him.

"My dagger!" He moved into the fringe of the quicksand,
his boots sinking up to the ankles as he hunted with his eyes.

"Bardolph, leave it go!"

" 'Tis gold-plated and the hilt of three-quarters precious,
finely worked and honed by Anast the Elder, Torquil."

"Yes. I've seen it and I know it's your pride, man, but
consider what—"

Bardolph didn't hear him, but let out an excited exclama-
tion as he spotted a faint gleam disappearing in the sand.
"There it is!" He dove for the flash of light, spread-eagling
himself as he leaped.

"Idiot!" Torquil extended himself into the quicksand and
managed to keep his footing as Bardolph flailed about until he
triumphantly held the dagger aloft. This time the bandit
leader had to work twice as hard to free his follower from the
pit. Bardolph emerged covered with grime but the dagger
glowed in the dim light.

"Beautiful," Bardolph said reverently as he began to clean
the blade. "I couldn't let it go."

"Not as beautiful as a life," Torquil growled at him. He
nodded toward the blade. "The world is full of daggers. Too
many, I sometimes think. Perhaps it would be a safer place if
all were forbidden to own them."

"Don't be a fool, Torquil. Daggers do no harm. That lies
only in the hearts of those who wield them."

"Perhaps. Next time you would do well to let this one
go."

"Nay, there are none so beautiful as this one. I sometimes
feel sorry for the noble I stole it from." He slipped the
shining blade back into its sheath.

"It'll end up killing you someday." Bardolph only grinned at his leader.

Meanwhile Colwyn had rescued the dour Kegan, and the cyclops had easily freed Rhun. All stood safe again on firm ground.

But Colwyn was not satisfied. "Something's wrong," he muttered as he watched Rhun thanking the giant. He studied the little band. Surely they were still one short? Wouldn't Torquil notice an absence? But the bandit chief was arguing with Bardolph over something.

Then the face returned to him and a name to match it. He looked carefully at the fringe of the quicksand pit, at the places concealed by overhanging bushes and roots.

"Menno!" he shouted, spotting a waving hand.

The unfortunate thief had swallowed more than one mouthful of quicksand, which had prevented him from shouting for help. Colwyn unhesitatingly splashed toward him, slowing only when his own legs began to vanish into the muck. The quicksand was especially treacherous and he could feel himself sliding into the bottomless ooze even as he flattened himself on the slick surface and extended his right hand. Menno's flailing fingers barely managed to lock with Colwyn's own.

The cyclops used Rhun and Oswyn as anchors while they in turn clung to Ergo and Torquil. With his retreat assured, he reached out and took Colwyn's left hand in an unbreakable grip.

But Menno had found the center of the quicksand pool and no matter how hard Colwyn pulled, the thief continued to sink. His eyes bugged wide as he strained to reach Colwyn with his other hand, but already his shoulders had slipped beneath the surface.

The veins stood out on Colwyn's neck as he strained with the effort of maintaining his hold. "Hang on, Menno!"

They were the last words the poor man heard. His fingers slipped free of Colwyn's. With a faint hissing sound he vanished beneath the surface. There weren't even any bubbles to mark his grave.

The cyclops had to use all his great strength to pull Colwyn clear of a like death. Every eye and hand was bent to the rescue effort.

So no one saw the visitor who approached the seer from behind. He was of similar height and dimensions. In fact, he was identical to the wise man in every respect save one. When he blinked, there was a definite crimson flash from his eyes.

The seer sensed the presence. "Is that you, Titch?"

The newcomer extended a hand and rested it gently on the nape of the seer's neck. "It is I, brother. Rest now."

The fingers clenched. The muscles that drove them were more than human. There was no compassion in that grasp, only efficiency. The seer let out a single, whispery gasp and then he was dead. No one saw the changeling slide the tired old body into the swamp. The Wyn-nah-Mabrug claimed another secret.

With a grunt the cyclops finally yanked Colwyn clear, stood him on shore.

"My thanks, friend." Colwyn's gaze returned to the place where Menno had vanished. The surface was once more calm and deceptive.

"No one could have saved him," Rell murmured.

"I had his hand. I had it in mine," Colwyn muttered. "I lost him."

"The swamp took him from you. Nobody lost him," said Torquil. "Menno would have been first to agree. Not twenty men could have pulled him clear, as deeply as he'd sunk. He'd found the center of the pit."

"The earth has a strong grip," Ynyr commented. "When

it wants someone badly enough there is nothing any mortal can do."

Colwyn considered as he stared at the hand that had so recently held that of a living man, a companion. Then he put the memory behind him. "We still have not gained what we came here for." He glanced toward the smallest member of his army. "Titch, how far to the temple?"

"Not far now," the boy assured him quietly. He looked to the seer for confirmation, but the seer appeared absorbed in a study of the swamp.

"Oswyn, stay here and make sure we're not being followed."

The thief looked uneasy. "I acknowledge you as king, Colwyn, but this is no royal court."

Torquil took a step toward him, fingering the hilt of his sword. "Are you so recently escaped from an early death that you're already anxious to tempt it again?"

"Easy," said a deep voice, interrupting. The cyclops looked down at Colwyn. "I will stay behind. I am used to solitude. Working alone will not trouble me."

"All right," Colwyn agreed, seeing the logic of the giant's words. Oswyn breathed a silent sigh of relief.

Colwyn moved to stand close to the seer. "I'll lead the seer. Titch, you take the lead."

"Thank you, brother," said the changeling in the seer's voice. He reached a hand toward Colwyn's shoulder.

It did not reach its goal. Torquil stepped between them. "I'll lead the old man, Colwyn. You go out in front with the boy."

The changeling's mastery of mimicry did not extend to expressing disappointment. It immediately shifted its groping paw to the bandit leader's shoulder and proceeded to ignore him. It had no interest in Torquil and kept its attention focused obtusely on Colwyn. In addition to inhuman strength it was possessed of inhuman patience. It could wait. The right time would present itself.

It always did.

As they continued onward, the terrain soon changed, revealing a second large lake off to their left. Colwyn was glad to see it, even though its predecessor had disgorged a band of Slayers. They would not be surprised like that again, and water was no trickster like quicksand. At least if they were forced into the lake they would be able to swim. Not like poor Menno.

They did not encounter any more quicksand, however. The ground remained soggy but no boot sank more than an inch into the surface. He thought of asking the seer or Titch how they'd lost the path and stumbled into the quicksand pit, then decided that even a seer could make mistakes. Obviously it had been a long time since the wise man had traveled this country, and swamps can shift themselves about with every change of seasons. It was a wonder they'd not encountered more troubles than they already had.

There was nothing to mark the place as special or chosen when they finally arrived. No monoliths, no graven images, no moss-covered walls. It presented the same aspect as the rest of the Great Swamp, but Titch immediately noticed something Colwyn and the others would have passed by.

"There." Torquil and the seer-that-was-not moved forward.

"We are in sight of the trees, brother."

Ahead and slightly to one side three trees emerged from the ground, their trunks pressing tight until they rose mist-ward as a single bole. Unusual but hardly unique, the sight would have gone unnoticed by anyone unfamiliar with its ancient meaning. Certainly Colwyn and Torquil would have marched on past without sparing the awkward growth a second look.

Staying long in one place always made the cyclops nervous. He liked to keep moving, and it had been some time

since his newfound companions had vanished ahead of him,
swallowed up by fog and distance. He'd remained behind to
guard the rear against nothing but mud, for nothing had
appeared that would demand his attention. Besides, there was
no telling what new dangers still lay ahead. His friends might
need his help again very soon.

So be it, he decided. He would continue to serve as rear
scout, but would interpret that order to suit his own nature.
Skirting the quicksand pit, he began to follow his friends'
footsteps, taking special care to give any body of water larger
than a bathtub a close inspection. He saw nothing more
dangerous than frogs and newts. There were no more Slayers
preparing watery ambush. He strained his ears and heard only
swamp sounds.

He was debating whether or not to increase his pace when
a faint rushing noise caught his attention. Odd tides caressed
the Great Swamp. Probably that was what had confused the
seer and Titch. In drier times of year, the quicksand pits
might not exist.

As he held his balance and watched, he saw the water
draining into some hidden cavern. As it did so, the source of
the peculiar slapping noise emerged from the shallows. Behind him, where quicksand had reclaimed dry land, the
muddy bridge across the treacherous bog was rising once
more. But there was something more, a different noise. Flesh
beating against the damp soil.

A limp arm swung over a second time to smack the mud.
The cyclops recognized Menno's shirt as the body was thrust
clear of the water. Too bad for the man. A rotten way to die.

Then his regrets turned to curiosity and his curiosity
quickly became fearful concern.

He hurried toward the newly emerged land bridge, not
caring if the earth suddenly chose to turn to quicksand again
beneath his boots. He knelt and turned the second body over,

only to find himself staring into the peaceful, silent face of the dead seer. But if the seer lay here by Menno, dead as the throat of an old fire-mountain, then who walked in his guise alongside the boy and the bandit leader?

Realization came with terrifying speed.

Like Colwyn, Torquil was searching for signs that this spot represented the end of their search. Like him, he found nothing.

"Are you sure this is the place, old man?"

"The boy will know," the changeling replied sibilantly.

Titch looked to his master. "We are in sight of the trees, brother."

Ynyr frowned as the silence stretched into minutes. He didn't understand his old friend's hesitation. Of course, he had no knowledge of the proper procedure to follow. Perhaps this contemplative pause on the part of the seer was how the enchantment began. Still, something didn't feel right to him. He kept his concern to himself, however. The seer is old. Give him time.

At last he spoke and Ynyr was able to relax.

"He who seeks the knowledge must lead me to the appointed place. No one else may approach. The magic is powerful. Have a care you all stand well back." Torquil and his men needed no further urging. They stepped several paces farther back from the tri-trunked tree.

Colwyn exchanged places with Torquil, waited until the seer had a comfortable grip on his shoulder. "How do I lead you, wise one?"

"Toward the trees, and away from your friends. Toward enlightenment, Colwyn of Turold."

Keeping a tight rein on his growing sense of excitement, Colwyn led the seer toward the trees. There was a faint trembling in the old man's wrist, and Colwyn thought that he too must be excited at what was to come.

Soon they had approached to within touching distance of the gnarled old bark. Colwyn halted. They'd distanced themselves considerably from the others and mist hid them from view.

"What happens now, wise one?"

"As I promised, enlightenment." The long, dexterous fingers slid gently upward, from shoulder to neck. "Here is the knowledge you seek."

The fingers started to tighten convulsively even as something in the seer's tone caused Colwyn to whirl. So fast did he twist, that the changeling's grip was not secured, the fingers not quite in place to snap the neck. But they did not fall away. Instead, they continued to contract around the startled Colwyn's neck even as he hammered desperately at the powerful arm.

Another second and Colwyn would die, his head forced back at an impossible angle by the changeling's inhuman strength. Another second . . . and the pressure vanished from Colwyn's throat.

He staggered for a moment, rubbing at his bruised neck and staring at the swaying figure of the seer-that-was-not even as he drew the knife at his belt. Stared at the seer's shoulder, now ragged and bloody.

Flung with enormous force by the onrushing Rell from a good fifty yards distant, the huge trident had ripped into the changeling's back. Staggering backward, the creature flailed at Colwyn. But now the intended victim was on guard.

Colwyn stepped forward and drove inward with his knife. No longer was it the image of the seer that he fought. That kindly, wise old visage was coming apart even as he fought it, even as the hand that had sought his throat had changed into a grotesque, groping claw.

The changeling stumbled about, screeching in frustration as
fluid gushed from its disintegrating skull. Colwyn did not
have to stab again, nor was the help of his hurrying friends
required. As he stared, the changeling collapsed and died in
the manner of such unnatural things.

Torquil moved to stand beside him as Colwyn rubbed at his
sore throat.

"You all right?"

"Well enough, thanks to our friend." He nodded toward
the approaching Rell. "If not for his strong arm, *that*"—and
he nodded at the rapidly decomposing alien corpse—"would
have snapped my neck."

"So perish all such manifestations of the Beast," Torquil
muttered grimly.

VIII

Titch was the last to arrive, pushing through the assembled men to gape at the body. "I don't understand," he murmured. He looked over at Ergo. "Where is the seer? The trident . . . his arm . . . I don't understand." As they watched, the body continued to decompose before their eyes, until at last there was only a stain of corruption against the clean earth.

Ergo put his arm around the boy. "I don't understand either, boy." He looked over at Ynyr. "Well, wise man? Explain what we've witnessed. Or can it be that in your wisdom, you too were deceived?"

"Well and truly deceived," said Ynyr sadly. "I feel as ignorant at this moment as a mudskipper. I should have seen through the deception. I thought something wrong but could not see it. Fool!" He shook his head angrily, incensed at his costly misperception.

"Neither I nor the seer anticipated this ploy of the Beast. I had thought that when we disposed of the Slayers who rose from the first lake to attack us that we had succeeded in defeating his evil intentions. Clearly that was not so. Likely that attack was naught but a clever diversion, designed to make us look for swords and spears instead of weapons far more subtle and dangerous.''

"Some diversion," Ergo said with a snort. "We lost a good man . . . even if he was a thief and a cutthroat.''

"None of us threatens the Beast. It is Colwyn he fears and Colwyn he seeks to slay. The Beast has many weapons at his command. Among them are devices far more insidious than mere Slayers. This was one of them: a changeling.''

Titch understandably looked confused. "Then he who attacked Lord Colwyn was not my master?''

Ynyr shook his head. "No, boy. 'Twas a creature sent out in the guise of your master the seer, who was my friend, to dupe us until it could wreak the Beast's will upon young Colwyn. The Beast is a master manipulator of false souls, so to change mere faces and bodies is but child's play to him. From now on we must be on our guard against a repetition of such deceptions, though I think we may be safe from such manifestations for a little while. The Beast does not like to reuse methods recently encountered.'' He turned his gaze to the cyclops. Rell stood nearby, still fighting to regain his wind after his long, desperate sprint.

"How did you know, one-eye? I but suspected that something was amiss, but you divined it.''

Rell favored them with a half-smile. "Would that I could claim such a talent. Nay, I was but checking our rear when the swamp disgorged the seer's body alongside Menno's. The quicksand buckles and heaves like a fat man's stomach. It did so barely in time to reveal truth to me.

"I came as fast as I could. If I had been but a little faster we might not have lost the chance to locate the temple."

"And if you had been a step slower or less accurate in your throw, we might not have reason left to regret the loss," Ynyr told him firmly. "We are all in your debt."

"What is this talk of debts?" Colwyn joined the discussion. Behind him, Torquil and Kegan continued to exchange mutual recriminations for not spotting the deceiver, while the rest of the men argued among themselves.

"Specifically of one debt," Ynyr explained, "which all owe to Rell for saving your life."

"Already I owe much to many, and still we have not reached the end of our journey." He extended a hand. "This will have to serve as my thanks for now, since it is all I have to offer."

The cyclops smiled as he took Colwyn's hand in his own. "Gold is common, friendship is not. This is thanks enough."

"May it shine as brightly. What of the real seer?"

"Dead, as I've said. Back in the swamp by the quicksand."

"He gave his life for us," Colwyn murmured, "trying to aid us in our journey."

"He was my only family," said the downcast Titch. "I never knew my father or mother. He was both to me, and teacher as well."

"We're your family now, boy," said Colwyn gently.

Ergo took the lad aside. Titch was struggling not to cry. He did not succeed. Colwyn forced himself to turn from the sound of weeping to confer with Ynyr and Torquil. He had listened too much to weeping lately.

"We have plans to make. We have no way of finding the

Black Fortress. With the seer dead and the temple submerged, our window on the Beast has been broken.''

Ynyr nodded thoughtfully. ''So it would appear.''

''Then what are we to do?''

Ynyr considered. When he spoke again it was with evident reluctance. ''There is one other way of locating the Fortress, if the one I have in mind will help us. She sees without the aid of devices, a gift of breeding.'' He threw Colwyn an odd look as he said this, but Colwyn was not of a mind to question the old man's thoughts.

''You speak of another seer?''

''Not precisely another seer, no. Someone . . . different.''

''And who might that be?''

''The widow of the web.''

Torquil turned to spit disgustedly. ''That creature helps no one, except to help them to a quick and horrible death. None who go there return.''

''It is not she who is to blame but the captor who keeps watch over her. The same captor that protects her from the attentions of Slayers as much as men. This creature makes no distinction between Slayers and supplicants, but destroys all who approach the widow with equal dispatch.''

''Nor will it make any special distinction for us,'' Torquil pointed out.

''She has great powers, the widow.''

''To kill,'' Torquil admitted readily.

''She may not kill me, for I know her name.''

''That's no secret. Her name is death. A name I would not call out no matter how great my need.''

''No. I mean her real name, her true name. An old and powerful name still respected today.''

Colwyn looked doubtful. ''It sounds too dangerous, Ynyr.

I value your council too highly to let you risk your life for
a vision that may not be granted.''

"I must try. We all risk our lives on this journey. My
risk is no greater than yours." He smiled knowingly. "And
I have less life to lose. I sometimes think I have lived too
long already. As for my counsel that you value so highly, it
would be of little use to you if we were to spend years
wandering aimlessly about in search of the Fortress. You
need to find and penetrate it quickly, before the Beast has
time to devise defenses to keep you out. By moving as fast
as we have we keep him a little off balance, a touch
uncertain. Thus he cannot focus his powers as effectively
as he otherwise might.''

Torquil looked away. "So we keep him off balance, eh?
Tell that to the seer, or to Darro and Menno.''

"You have no comprehension of the forces the Beast could
bring to bear on us if given time.''

"And I'd like to keep it that way, old man!" He turned and
stalked away from them.

"He discounts our need," said Ynyr.

"He's frightened, that's all," Colwyn countered. "I'm
frightened, too.''

"It is no vice to be human. I *must* try to obtain the
widow's help, Colwyn. I can think of no other way to locate
the Fortress quickly. We cannot chance stumbling upon it by
accident or luck. We do not have that much time. And Lyssa
certainly does not.

"You say that you value my counsel. I counsel this
approach. You cannot value what I say in one breath and
disregard what I recommend in the next.''

"I see what Torquil means about your twisting words."
Colwyn's expression was grim. "Very well. If you're sure
this is the only choice remaining to us . . .''

"It is, my boy, it is. I wish it were otherwise. I wish it

more than you can imagine, for reasons that have nothing to
do with the real risk to my person. But each must do what
each can do. Perhaps it was preordained.''

"You told me once you didn't believe in that.''

"So I did.'' Ynyr gave him a pleased smile. "You
remember. A good virtue for a king. But it seems too much
of a coincidence that I should be compelled to visit the
widow.''

Colwyn wanted to know what the old man meant, but he
held his questions. Some things were meant not to be pried
into.

It was hard to imagine a more cheerful morning or a more
pleasing sight than the evergreen woods that greeted them
upon their emergence from the Wyn-nah-Mabrug. Torquil
inhaled deeply of the fresh, pine-scented air and turned to spit
back at the swampland they'd just abandoned.

"And may I never set foot in such a country again as long
as I live!''

"I'll second that,'' said Kegan readily. "I dislike traveling
where the air itself is an ally of one's enemies. Let it keep its
secrets. I've no desire to visit the place again, no matter what
treasure sunken temples may hold.''

Only Rell did not join in the chorus of relief. Fog and mist
had been friend to him all his life. Someday, when this quest
was ended, he hoped to rejoin them. He gave little weight to
this Colwyn's protestations of friendship. As he'd learned
more than once, in clear air and on full bellies, politicians
tended to forget awkward promises made during more trying
times.

Possibly I misjudge this one, though, he thought. Perhaps
he means what he says. Not that it mattered. Better to live as
a pessimist. That way one was rarely disappointed.

He looked down at the small boy who clung tightly to
his huge hand. The child was handling his fate better than

many adults. One could almost imagine him a young of the one-eyes, so stoic was his attitude and solemn his composure. Rell wished he could do something for Titch but he could not think of anything. Friendship was all he had to offer.

Ergo trailed behind, rummaging through his pockets, glancing intently at one scrap of paper after another before jamming them back into their cloth repositories.

"Blast! One of these days I've got to get organized. Hire a scribe to rewrite everything nice and neat. Ah." He smiled at nothing in particular, dropped slightly to one side of the marchers. No one saw him melt into the bushes.

Oswyn hesitated, hand on sword hilt. Kegan trotted up to stand next to him.

"What is it?"

Oswyn stared into the trees. "I thought I heard something."

His companion joined him in listening hard. "I hear nothing. What did it sound like?"

"I don't know. Strange. A popping sound."

Kegan listened a moment longer, then shrugged. "A branch falling off a tree, a hare breaking twigs. You see Slayers beneath every bush."

"Is that so surprising?"

"I suppose not. Not when I've started to see them rising from every creek and pond we pass."

"Aye." Oswyn let his hand slip from his sword. "It must have been a branch."

A small brown shape had been watching the two men closely. Now it padded on ahead, then cut back toward the troupe. It halted before the startled Titch, who picked it up instinctively.

Rell eyed the puppy uncertainly. "Now where did that little

dust mote come from?'' He turned and scanned the forest.
There was no sign of passing travelers or nearby habitation.

"I don't care," said Titch delightedly. "Hey, stop that!"
The puppy yapped softly and continued to lick the boy's
face.

Colwyn heard the excitement and slowed to join them.
"Now that's a cute little mouse." He frowned, looked over
their heads. "Where's Ergo?"

"He's—" Titch started to say, but a growl from the puppy
made him hesitate. Or perhaps it was something he saw in the
dog's eyes.

"He'll be back real soon," Titch finished. The puppy
resumed licking his nose. "Can I keep him?"

"Hmmm?" Colwyn murmured absently, still searching the
forest. His attention came back to the ball of brown fluff in
the boy's arms. "Of course. Just keep him quiet."

"I will," Titch promised. The puppy promptly curled up
and went to sleep in his arms.

Oswyn found himself leaning back, craning his neck to
locate the sky. "Never have I seen woods like these! Heard of
'em, but never thought to see them. These trees are like
castles."

"Which they are, to the many creatures who inhabit their
upper reaches," Ynyr explained as they passed around one
particularly enormous bole. Overhead it was a long way to
the vault of heaven, but there was none of the claustrophobic
feeling that had enveloped them all during their trek through
the swamps.

"Peaceful place," Oswyn added.

"Not up that way." Ynyr brought them to a halt and
pointed.

Through a break in the towering woods they could see a
sloping cliff of dark basalt. It was a difficult climb, but not an
impossible one. The widow's mountain.

Ynyr turned to face Colwyn. "Here we must part company, my friend."

Colwyn shook his head. "Not yet. I'm going with you. I can help." He touched the strap holding the glaive.

Ynyr only smiled. "No. The glaive's power is great, but it is not limitless. You must retain it for when it will truly be needed." He indicated the slope ahead. "Besides, if two approach, it is likely that both will die. There will be very little time in which to make contact and when I present myself to the widow there must be no chance of a misunderstanding. Your presence and the need to explain it would only hamper my efforts, Colwyn. Alone, I may have a chance."

Torquil had listened quietly. Now he offered his own advice to Colwyn. "Each to his chosen fate. Listen to the wise man."

"Yes, listen. As I've tried to teach you to do. Each to his fate. If I have not returned by tomorrow morning, you will know mine."

"And if that should happen, what then? How am I to proceed without your good advice?"

"You must go on as best you are able, my boy. That is *your* fate." He conjured up a smile. "It is too early for despair. Everything may go as hoped. Meanwhile get some rest and try to ease your mind as well as your body." He turned away and set off toward the dark cliff.

"Now that's the advice of a wise man," commented Kegan. He proceeded to find himself a soft spot near a great twisted root and sit down. Torquil chose a resting place opposite.

"Wait, boy," Titch was yelling, "wait for me!" The puppy had jumped from his arms and was scampering into the bushes.

Ergo reappeared a moment later. He paused a moment to

scratch behind one ear, frowned, then joined the boy. Rell looked on amusedly, understanding now what he'd only been able to suppose earlier. Titch looked disappointed, but not gravely so.

"I still say it's a foolish wish," Ergo said to the lad. "I thought to show you that. Well, don't you agree with me now?"

Titch shuffled his feet, staring at the ground. "You're a nice friend, Ergo, but if you want the truth . . ."

"Careful, boy," Rell warned him. "The truth can be dangerous."

Titch didn't care. "I liked you better as a puppy."

"Fagh! Children!" Ergo walked away, shaking his head bemusedly and hunting for a place to relax. He was exhausted, and not just from the strain of transformation.

Colwyn took note of his condition as well as that of the others and beckoned Torquil over.

"We have no food save what little remains in our packs and the men are too tired to hunt. I can't blame them. These past days would have tried the endurance of a hundred men. Right now I confess to little enthusiasm for killing anything, even a deer."

"What do you want from me, Colwyn?"

"Suggestions. You've roamed this country while I've been stuck in a castle learning history and administration. Those are of little use on an empty belly. If you've a talent for scavenging, man, use it now."

Torquil rubbed the stubble of beard that decorated his chin. "Well now, sir, that presents something of a problem. What we call scavenging you might call by another name."

"Promise payment in the name of Turold and Eirig," Colwyn told him.

"No disrespect intended, sir, but common folk are disinclined to trust the promises of princes, having been lied to by them so often in the past.''

"Don't deal me homilies, Torquil. I'm too tired and too hungry. The fate of Krull itself hangs in the balance.'' He turned to gaze at the distant mountain, which had swallowed up his most trusted adviser.

"Your pardon, Colwyn, but I did not mean to tease you, though I'd appreciate it if you didn't play so loose with the word *hang* in my presence. It makes my men and me nervous. Are you saying that we should obtain what victuals we can by any means necessary?''

"I would prefer that you not break the law while doing so, if that's what you mean.''

"Now that will be difficult, not to mention different. But there may be a way. Hunger has a way of stimulating a man's mind as well as his inventiveness.'' He turned and shouted. "Kegan!''

The thief pushed back his hair. "Now what? Another crisis?''

"None greater than a score of empty bellies. Get your lazy tail over here.''

Grumbling to himself, Kegan climbed to his feet and ambled over. Colwyn explained the predicament.

"I thought as much. At least, my guts did. So it's up to poor old Kegan to feed this lot, is it?''

"You're as supple with words as most thieves are with their fingers, Kegan,'' said Torquil. "We're in no shape to outrun the local law even if we had the time to lead them a merry chase. I blush to confess it but we must resort to legal means of feeding ourselves.''

"How do you expect me to manage this miracle?'' Kegan asked curiously. "I'm no wise man. That one's gone up the mountain to seek his death. Better you'd thought to have him feed us first. Starving men make poor mourners.''

"You're not using your head, man. A common enough occurrence when tired and hungry. Think! Doesn't one of your wives live in a village near here? You and I have traveled close by this giant wood before.''

Kegan became a study in concentration. "Let me see. Lona. No, she moved with her family down to the Hyrwyn River country. Pity. Such a gentle, sweet girl, gifted with such superb—''

"Don't drift, man. You're not that hungry, but we all will be soon if you don't use your head.''

"Sorry.'' Kegan gave them an apologetic smile and concentrated again. "There's Imrone, but she's in Uvghern, and that's leagues from here.''

Colwyn leaned close to Torquil, whispering. "How many wives does he have? Or is he boasting for my benefit?''

Torquil pursed his lips. "Kegan is not one of those men who need to boast. He is quiet and most reluctant to discuss the subject. I think it embarrasses him. As to your question of wives, I believe the total stands at seven or eight at last count. They come and go and sometimes 'tis difficult for the poor fellow to remember which ones he's married to and which he's only courting.

"I recall one time in Mulleen Towne when he spent an entire evening charming this beautiful if drunken lass, only to discover the next morning that he'd married her the previous year.''

"She must have been furious.''

"Not really. She'd forgotten that she'd married *him,* so ignorance in this instance became the mother of romance and they enjoyed a fine reunion. Kegan's a traveling man, you see.''

Colwyn nodded, forcing himself to repress a smile. "He covers a lot of ground."

"Aye," agreed Torquil, with a touch of envy in his tone, "and that's not all."

"Merith!" Kegan said suddenly. "She lives in Torunj, a village crowding the northern flank of this forest."

Torquil looked satisfied, glanced briefly at Colwyn as if to say "I told you so," and spoke to Kegan: "I'm sure she's beautiful and charming, but can she cook?"

Kegan struggled to remember. "As I recall it's not her strongest point."

"Well, just have her bring provisions ." He looked past his companion. "His Magnificence has told me he can cook. We'll soon see."

"When did he lay claim to that particular talent?" Colwyn wondered. "I never heard him say anything about it."

"You've been fortunate to lead us, Colwyn, while I've been stuck back in the pack with him whose mouth is half as big as his face. Aye, he said he could cook, along with being master of half a dozen other abilities. Too many to pack into so slight a frame, if you ask me, but perhaps this claim was a little less of a lie than the rest." He turned and strolled back to confront the resting Ergo.

"You once told me that you could cook, befriender of small children."

"And so I can."

"Well then, O genius of giblets, your hour has arrived. You will be given the chance to make magic with a cauldron."

Ergo looked surprised, then downright pleased. "You're bringing me a deer. Ah, tenderloin of venison! Flank steak roasts. We will eat like kings."

"Not likely," Torquil informed him. "More like serfs.

Oatmeal and, if we're fortunate, some small game. Maybe some vegetables if the Slayers haven't burned all the fields hereabouts.''

''Food for crows!'' Ergo's initial enthusiasm dimmed quickly.

''True . . . in the hands of an ordinary man. But you, O wizard of the spatula, surely you can make small game taste like venison? Any fool can cook a deer, but it would take a true genius to make table-gold from cellar-lead. You *can* perform this simple bit of magic. Or can you?''

Ergo was aware that Torquil's gaze wasn't the only one focused on him. Kegan was watching from his position behind the bandit chief and Oswyn looked on interestedly from his resting place. Titch's eyes were wide and even Colwyn looked intrigued.

With such an audience he could hardly turn down the challenge. He drew himself up. ''If I choose, bumpkin, I can make your *boot* taste like venison. Fetch me wood for a fire. Good dry wood, no green branches, and plenty of loose bark, cleansed of insects. And whatever fragrant leaves you can glean from the forest floor.''

Torquil grinned, genuflected mockingly. ''As you wish, Magnificence.''

Ergo talked to himself as he inspected the campsite. ''Now then; fire there, beneath that small tree. I can hang the game from a stick set between those two branches and that root. Back the root with some rocks and we'll have a good place for baking potatoes. Then put the—'' He broke off, staring. Titch and Rell were heading off into the woods. He chased after them.

''Wait! Where are you going, you mismatched mongrels? I need your help.''

Titch turned and spoke firmly. ''We have things of our own to attend to. Important things.''

"More important than helping me with dinner?" Titch nodded. "Well then, dinner will have to wait. I will come with you."

"No," Rell told him. "You have a lot of work to do, preparing the fire and then our food. How can you think of leaving with so many depending on your work?"

"My work can wait and so can the meal." He frowned at them. "What are you two up to?"

"Our own business," Rell replied with maddening indifference. "Nothing that need concern you."

"Is that the way to treat a companion? I thought we were friends, Rell."

"We are. But you can't come." He looked down, put a hand on Titch's head and tousled the boy's hair. "Come, little one, we have *important* work to do."

They strolled off together, Rell bending low so Titch could whisper in his ear. Try as he might, Ergo couldn't escape the feeling that they were talking about him.

All right, let them gossip. He angrily turned back toward camp. Friends who whisper about a man behind his back are no friends at all. He kicked at the ground.

"Some friends. Never trust a boy whose main desire in life is to care for some dirty mutt, nor a man who looks at life through a keyhole."

Maybe they'd be late for the meal. In that case they'd miss the unique feast he would prepare. That would show 'em. He began clearing the site for the fire, planning in his mind a meal fit for the palate of the most discerning gourmet. It did not trouble him that he was likely to be half a hundred ingredients shy of the means to concoct such a supper, and it served to keep his mind from the mystery his erstwhile friends had embarked upon.

"I know they were back here somewhere," Titch was muttering as he led the cyclops deeper into the forest. The

moon was rising and it barely shed enough light to show the
way through the massive trees. But Titch wasn't relying on
mere light to guide him. Living all his life with the seer had
taught him to use all his senses. Now his nose began to twitch
as they penetrated still darker woods.

"I hope you're right about this, boy." Rell brushed a
thorny branch aside. "Otherwise we're going to look like a
grand pair of fools when we return."

"I was sure of it, Rell. I couldn't mistake—" He stopped
and pointed. "There, you see!"

Rell moved forward, took a moment to gaze in awe at the
sight before them before reaching back to pat the boy on the
head. "I ask forgiveness for doubting you, Titch. You may be
small in stature but you've the senses of a wolf."

"The seer used to say I was a little like a wolf cub."
Thoughts of the seer made him sad, and he hurried to turn his
mind to more pleasant thoughts. Never linger over past
misfortunes, the old man had always told him. The past is
dead. Only the future lives on.

"Boost me up," he ordered Rell. The cyclops knelt and
picked him up in one hand, held him high.

"How do such wondrous fruits come to grow here?" Rell
murmured.

"The trees around us are giants. So are the bushes,"
observed Titch as he considered where to begin. "Why not
these as well?" He reached out and plucked a single gooseberry from a near branch. It was only slightly smaller than his
head.

"Ergo the Magnificent has a large mouth, but he won't
know what to say about this. He'll have a hard time stuffing
these in his pocket."

Rell took down the first berry, set it gently on the ground so
as not to bruise the delicate skin. "But not so hard stuffing
them in his stomach."

"We'll need some other things, too. I guess we'll have to go into that village."

"Yes," Rell agreed, "and we'll have to be quiet about it. I don't think my presence would be reassuring to the townsfolk."

The White Castle as it appears when Prince Colwyn first arrives to meet his bride-to-be Princess Lyssa.

Princess Lyssa (Lysette Anthony) and Prince Colwyn (Ken Marshall) reflected in the fount before which they exchange wedding vows.

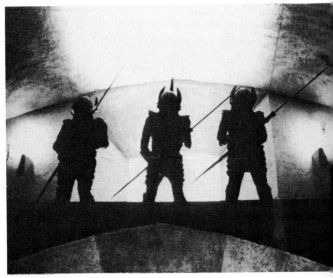

Silhouetted in the Armoury Archway of the White Castle, three
Slayers prepare to abduct Princess Lyssa as she is fleeing to an
underground tunnel.

Slayers move up the stairway of the White Castle while attacking royal men-at-arms at the beginning of the big massacre.

A Slayer sends a neon spear into a wagon inside the courtyard of the White Castle just after the massacre.

Prince Colwyn holds the mystical Glaive, a key to the extraordinary power required to defend his world against all odds.

Prince Colwyn and Ynyr (Freddie Jones) watch in fascination as the Seer (John Welsh) tries to locate the Black Fortress by calling forth the powers of his spinning Emerald.

The Black Fortress, home of the Beast and his Slayers, appears in a desolate landscape of the planet Krull.

Rell, the Cyclops (Bernard Bresslaw), with his mighty trident in hand, watches out for dangers while Colwyn and his men travel across the treacherous Great Swamp.

Colwyn and his army are bombarded by the Slayers' neon spears as they travel across the Great Swamp.

**Ynyr scrambles desperately through the webbed cave of the Widow,
seeking her cocoon before the Crystal Spider takes his life.**

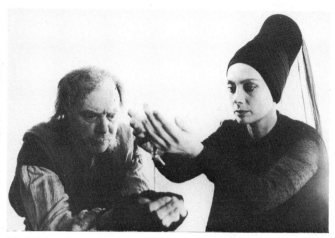

The Widow of the Web (Francesca Annis) transforms into the beautiful young woman Ynyr remembers and pours the sands of her life into her lover's hands.

The lethal Crystal Spider destroys the Widow's Cocoon after Ynyr has departed.

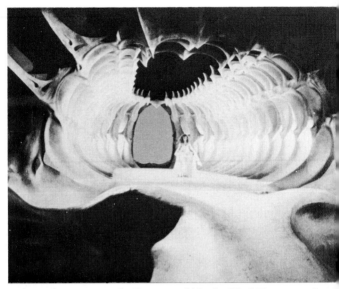

Princess Lyssa enters the Hexagon within the Black Fortress, only to have the structure close around her.

The Beast as he appears to Lyssa inside the Black Fortress.

Princess Lyssa in the Hexagon confronts another of the Beast's attempts to seduce her: a gold robe and crown.

Having lassoed his spirited Firemare, Prince Colwyn tries to control the horse with the help of Rell, the Cyclops.

Prince Colwyn and his army gaze in awe and fear at the Black Fortress as they draw nearer to the Iron Desert.

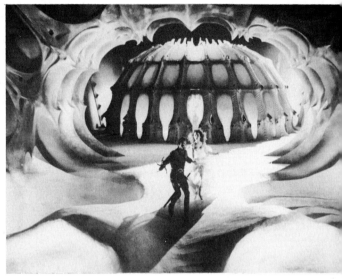

Prince Colwyn and Princess Lyssa flee from the Hexagon, the center of the Beast's power.

As the Beast draws nearer, Colwyn grips the Glaive and prepares to confront him outside the Hexagon.

As the Black Fortress begins to crumble, Lyssa, Colwyn, Torquil (Alun Armstrong), find Titch (Graham McGrath) and the wounded Ergo (David Battley) in the Fortress's underground chamber.

Having survived the destruction of the Black Fortress and now safe in the Grassy Valley are Torquil, Colwyn, Lyssa, Ergo and Oswyn (Todd Carty).

IX

The mountain seemed familiar to Ynyr but he didn't dwell on old memories as he skirted the dark boulders and basalt columns. The climb was the least of his concerns. So much hinged on the success of his application, yet he had no way of predicting how he would be received. This was a visit he would have preferred to have avoided, but with the death of the seer and the loss of the temple, no other course lay open to him and his companions.

Perhaps, given time, he might have seen another way, but time was growing short for Colwyn and Lyssa, and for Krull. If this opportunity was lost another might not arise for generations. He'd seen too much of what the Slayers were capable of. It was not right that humans should cower before a tyrant as capricious as the Beast. The work of generations was nearing fruition. What mattered his life compared to the lives of all the wise men and women who had striven before him to raise the possibility that hung just beyond their grasp?

So he was calm enough as he ascended the mountain, but he was glad Colwyn and the others were not along to see his fear. . . .

The stewpot was no enchanted caldron and the large wooden spoon wielded by a glum Ergo no magic wand, but to the hungry men settled beneath the towering trees the stew bordered on the miraculous. It was edible, and they would settle for that.

So many ingredients missing, Ergo thought sadly as he gazed into the bubbling pot! How do they expect me to produce a decent meal with stringy meat and old vegetables, and next to nothing in the way of spices? He hoped they appreciated his efforts. He did not consider the preparation of food beneath his wizardly station. Concocting a good meal often involved the use of the arcane arts, and this stew was no exception. Without his special abilities he doubted it would have turned out fit for human consumption.

The first spoonful, however, had been greeted by something less than universal applause. On the other hand, no one had yet thrown up. He expected nothing else. Country bumpkins have no appreciation for real cooking, he knew. Ah well, there would come another day when they'd have even less to eat. Then they'd remember his cuisine with fondness.

The peasant girl who served the stew to the travelers called herself Vella. Her clothes had seen better days, from her worn shoes to the battered kerchief that bound up her hair and the cloak that covered her slim form. Kitchen soot smudged her face, hiding the fact that she was considerably more attractive than a casual first glance would indicate.

No such ambivalence marred Merith's appearance. Her plain attire could not conceal her beauty. The men observed her admiringly as she made her way around the campsite,

introducing herself to each man before finally taking a bowl
of steaming stew to Kegan and sitting down beside him.

"You don't write as often as you should," she said
accusingly.

"Often enough." He shoveled in the stew—if you downed
it quickly it didn't taste so bad. "Consider how poorly I write
and how slowly you read." He smiled, ran a teasing hand
along her thigh. "I could have myself a fine time between the
time you started reading a letter and finally finished it."

"Which I could not do at all if so distracted by you," she
murmured softly. "Still, I wish that I could see more of you.
Then I wouldn't need to complain about nonexistent letters."

"I wish the same, m'love, but business requires that I
move about frequently. Birds and money both migrate with
the seasons."

"It seems that your travels bring you this way less and
less, Kegan."

"I have no control over my movements. Thanks to sheriffs
and bounty hunters. Nor do I work alone." He waved the
spoon in the general direction of his companions. "Torquil is
leader of this band and 'tis he who decides which land we
harvest next. I follow his orders." He smiled apologetically.
"So you see, it's out of my hands."

"It need not be, if you'd stay closer."

"Never tease a man when he's eating, love. It's bad for the
digestion. And don't pout. You're no little girl and I'm
certainly no wide-eyed little boy."

Merith let out a disappointed sigh. "You have an answer
for everything, Kegan."

"A necessary talent in my profession." He nodded across
the clearing at where Vella was serving a grateful Oswyn.
"Who's the girl? I don't recall seeing her around the village
the last time I was here."

"A sad tale brought her to us," Merith explained. "Poor

little thing. She staggered into the square one day, wearing less than you see on her now. Her village was burned by the Slayers. She said she wandered aimlessly about the countryside a long time before finding us. She had no place to go, no relatives left alive, no friends. So I took her in.''

"You have a big heart, Merith."

She slapped playfully at his hand. "Which cannot be measured by one's fingers. And you look at her like that one more time and I will cast her out."

"Merith, my sweet, she doesn't hold a candle to you. Look at her, filthy and stooped. Far too childlike for my taste. She's not even pretty."

"Do you think I would have brought her here for you to see if she was?"

Kegan laughed. "Dearest, you spend too many hours of the night worrying. Faithful is my middle name."

"Yes, faithful to whoever you're lying with at the moment. And if you were with me, those long hours of the night would not seem half so long."

He set his empty bowl aside and rested his head in her lap. "Someday I will tire of such work, m'love. But I am no farmer, no tradesman to sit every rest day in the marketplace and chatter about the crops with old men."

"I'd travel the country with you. All you'd have to do is ask."

"And I'd love to have you with me, and so would every other lonely wayfarer who keeps to the back trails. Too dangerous and too troublesome, Merith. I've told you that before."

Not to mention fatal, he thought, if she were to encounter any of the "cousins" he was forced to obliquely allude to when she discovered this or that item of feminine origin attached to his person.

"Let us not spend what time we have together regretting

the time we do not have." He pulled her face down to his and she did not resist.

Torquil made a face, spat a piece of unchewable gristle onto his spoon and heaved it into the woods. "You are true to your word, O sorceror of the saucepan," he shouted at their chef. "This stew tastes like my boot."

"Your stomach seems to handle it better than your mouth," Ergo snapped back.

"My stomach has no choice in the matter. My mouth does. Keeping a man alive is mere drudgery. Making him enjoy the process is called cooking."

"*You* try making something tasty out of this sludge," Ergo challenged him.

"Nay, my talents lie elsewhere, Magnificence."

"Then, do not presume to criticize those who have the use of such talent."

"I would not, if I could detect any evidence of such a talent in my bowl!"

Ergo turned away from the chuckles of his companions to stare disconsolately at the remaining stew. "So much for appreciating one's efforts. Well, it seems I've already lost two friends. I suppose this meal will lose me the rest of them." He gave the side of the caldron a vicious whack with his stirring spoon. "If only I had some spices!" He'd tried cursing the concoction but that didn't seem to have pepped it up. Nor did hot fudge sauce sound like the thing to complement wild game stew.

Colwyn leaned against the side of a normal-sized tree. It was a mere sapling in the giant forest. He chewed nervously on a much-worried thumbnail as he stared toward the crest of the dark mountain.

Ynyr was up there someplace, alone, likely walking toward his death. He'd listened to the wise man's words and understood the wisdom of them, but he still couldn't help feeling that he'd be of more use up there on the rocks instead of down in the forest, safe and unthreatened.

Yet Ynyr had ordered him to remain behind and remain he would . . . but he chafed anxiously at the restriction.

A hand touched his sleeve and he started, relaxing when he saw who it was. That young girl who'd come from the village to help Kegan's woman . . . Tella—no, Vella her name was.

She carried a bowl of hot stew and held it out to him. Her voice was soft, soothing. "You must eat something."

"I'm not hungry."

"Of course you are hungry." She gestured behind her. "All the others are hungry, so you must be hungry, too."

He smiled down at her. "Your logic is as simple as your dress."

She looked down at her attire and smiled back at him. "I would that I could look like a fancy court lady, but such is not my destiny."

"Never mind," he told her, "you look just fine."

"Then if my appearance pleases you, please eat something. For me?"

"I've done more for lesser beings. All right, I *am* hungry. Thank you." He accepted the bowl. "Do you forgive me for lying to you about my appetite?"

He was teasing her, but she took his words seriously. "Sometimes a man can carry such a burden that he forgets the needs of his body." She was eyeing him intently now, blue eyes burning from behind the mask of soot and dirt. "I forgive you, Colwyn."

He smiled uncertainly at her, then sat down. Still glancing occasionally up at the mountain, he devoured the stew. She took a seat nearby and watched him. When he was almost finished, he gave her a curious look.

"Don't you have anything else to do except sit there and watch me eat?"

She shrugged. "I do what Merith asks of me. She asks nothing of me now. She is busy enough with matters of her own." Colwyn looked past her but could see no sign of Kegan or Merith. Their absence spoke volumes, or at least a modest number of pages.

"You're a funny little thing."

"That's what the people in the village tell me. I try to keep out of their way. No one bothers me. Are you a real king?"

He grinned. "By accident of birth that is my lot, yes. It's nothing to boast of. None of us can help what we are born into. Mere chance seems an unfair way to begin existence."

"Yes, it does," she said with more solemnity than he'd expected. "I had not thought of it that way before."

Ergo had seen Merith and Kegan vanish into the woods. Now he watched as Vella sidled close to Colwyn. He cursed his luck along with the stew. It suddenly occurred to him that he'd been so busy feeding everyone else that he'd not had time to eat himself.

Bending over the pot, he inspected the remaining stew, selected a healthy mouthful with the stirring spoon and downed it. After a moment's reflective chewing, he grimaced, looked around to make sure no one was watching him, and slung the rest of the spoonful into a helpless bush, muttering to himself.

"The foul filcher was right. It does taste like his boot."

Before long only the remnants of the cooking fire illuminated the camp, mixed with what moonlight filtered down through the great trees. Bushes moved and several figures stealthily approached the sleeping camp. A tall shape moved silently among them, gently awakening Torquil, Kegan and Oswyn, motioning the startled men to silence as they awoke. They restrained their curiosity as they followed Rell back into the forest, knowing that their unvoiced questions would be answered soon.

Several minutes later Titch appeared, stole across the grass until he stood alongside the recumbent Ergo. He tapped the exhausted cook on the shoulder.

Ergo rolled over, blinked. "Oh, so it's you. Come back with your tail between your legs, eh? Well I'm not having any of it." He shook the boy's hand off and turned away from him. "Leave me alone. Go back to your one-eyed friend. Friends do not keep secrets from each other."

"Sometimes it's necessary," the boy said.

Ergo's reply was slick with sarcasm. "Did your wonderful seer tell you that?"

"No. I figured it out for myself." He glanced backward, saw the three thieves and the cyclops emerge from the woods. Between them they carried a bloated, misshapen object of impressive but irregular dimensions. Titch nudged Ergo once again.

"Do you know what I think, chef to the unappreciative? I think your nose is asleep."

"Asleep?" Ergo let out a derisive snort. "This nose? This nose works day and night, ready to sniff out friends and potential enemies alike. This nose is attuned to the finest culinary works our civilization has produced. This nose has never loafed an hour in its life, a paragon among nostrils, possessed of an olfactory—" He stopped, inhaled sharply. "What?" He sniffed a second time, started to sit up.

"No. Impossible. This nose asleep while the ambrosial aroma of gooseberries fills the air?" He sat up the rest of the way, grabbed Titch hard by the shoulders. "Where are they, boy? Tell me where they are and I forgive you everything, from your insufferable precocity to your choice of companions—including myself."

"Take it easy." Titch grinned hugely, enjoying himself. He looked to his left and nodded. "They're right behind you."

Ergo turned, saw the three men and Rell standing next to a

gooseberry trifle. The vision was impossible, surreal, but Ergo's nose did not deceive him. The trifle stood eight feet high. In the moonlight and firelight it gleamed as brightly as the walls of the White Castle.

His voice was reduced to an awed whisper. "A gooseberry trifle as big as a house."

"A small house," Rell admitted modestly.

"Did you think I'd forgotten your wish?" Titch said pridefully. "After you'd granted mine, if only temporarily? Rell and I had to sneak into the village to find the rest of the ingredients, then build a cook-fire far enough away from here to conceal the smell of baking. Rell's a good cook."

"Comes of living alone with a large appetite," the cyclops informed them all.

"*I* smelled out the gooseberry bushes," Titch added.

"Prince of nostrils, emperor of odors. I will crown you myself, boy." Ergo's voice was unnaturally subdued. He was unable to take his eyes from the dream become reality. "A small house you say? And what do you think a small person lives in, foolish cyclops? How deceiving you two were! I never would have imagined you were leaving me behind to mope while you and the boy were off arranging my assassination."

Titch frowned. "Assassination?"

Ergo rose slowly. "Do you not think I'm going to eat myself to death this very night? Hah? A supreme end, fit only for a king or master chef. How can I thank you both? Mere words will not suffice."

Titch smiled shyly. "If you don't die, sir, I'd still like a puppy." But Ergo was beyond hearing. At last he would be one with the upper crust. He worshipfully approached the trifle. Never was there a pastry so inaptly named.

"Look at its beauty," he murmured. "Rell, you are not a cook. You are an architect of the kitchen for all that you use flour instead of cement and berries instead of wood. Look at its lines, its color, its beauty.''

Torquil stepped forward and held out a large spoon. ''Look at its insides.''

Ergo turned to him, held up both hands. ''No! Not yet. This moment must be made to last, for all that my stomach is threatening me. Let me hug and kiss it a little. Let me run my fingers over its lovely skin.''

Off to one side Oswyn shook his head sadly, whispered to Kegan. ''You'd think the man was going to make love to it instead of eat it.'' Kegan withheld comment.

Ergo strolled slowly around the trifle. When he did not speak again, Titch moved to follow him . . . and followed until he'd circled the trifle completely.

''He's gone! Has he turned himself into a puppy again?''

As if in response, Ergo's head ripped through the top of the trifle, his face awash in gooseberry juice and bits of pulp and pastry.

''Not gone, but going, for I am preparing to turn myself into a glutton. And if I should die before this night is done, write this for my epitaph: 'Here lies Ergo, who died with his lips on a gooseberry. His friends were true and his desserts were just!' '' He vanished back into the trifle's depths.

Oswyn took a step toward the monumental pastry. ''Do you think he'd object to my snatching a bite or two?''

''Nay,'' said Kegan confidentally, ''he owes us more than that after that leathery supper. Even if he turns himself into a horse he'll have trouble finishing this little tart.''

Time passed as sections of pastry disappeared down hungry throats. One by one the revelers fell away from the trifle, sated and content. Not surprisingly, Ergo was the last to concede. He fell through an opening that had been made in the crust, staggered over to a nearby clump of thick grass, and collapsed. His long, drawn-out moan echoed through the forest. Titch and Rell walked over to join him.

Their presence did nothing to quell the throbbing beneath his hands. "Ohhhh'. . . where is that wise man? I need his ministrations now!"

Titch pursed his lips as he studied his friend. "I fear you have gone beyond Ynyr's abilities."

"I fear I've gone beyond living," Ergo groaned pitifully. "It was that last gooseberry."

There was no sympathy in Rell's reply: "That last gooseberry weighed five pounds."

Ergo twisted painfully on the grass. "Torturer! You had to remind me, as if I was ignorant of the fact at the time. A thousand torments consume you both!"

Rell looked knowingly down at Titch. "Spoken like a true friend, wouldn't you say?" Titch nodded solemnly.

Ergo's distress was good for at least an hour's clever commentary from his companions. Then the joke began to weary. Lulled by the steady sound of Ergo's moans, one by one they drifted off into contented sleep.

Only Colwyn remained awake, leaning against his tree, staring up at the mountain. Only Colwyn—and the girl Vella. She sat nearby, watching him with preternatural intensity.

Ynyr saw the light before he saw the opening. It was a pale glow, so faint it seemed no more than a reflection of the moonlight from the rocks, but as he drew nearer he saw that it had nothing to do with the moon. The light came from inside the mountain, illuminating the wide, oval opening like the mouth of a monster lit from the throat. The image was upsetting and he discarded it.

The climb had been harder than he expected. Now he paused to gather his strength before entering the cave. Inside he would need all the energy he could muster, and more. The inhabitant of this solitary place would not be impressed by shouts. It would take more than big words and sonorous phrases for him to succeed here. It would take the *right* words.

Carefully he edged inward along the right-hand wall. The rock was cool to his touch. It was reassuring to have something solid to lean against in such a place, where nightmares became real and death was something you could taste in the back of your mouth.

Ahead the cavern was draped with white; thin ropes fashioned from cream, a milky maze whose appearance was deceptively soft. The softness was as deceptive as the elasticity. Each thin cable was stronger than steel.

Ynyr slowed, reluctant to leave the comparative safety of the entrance. His gaze traveled to the center of the immense spiderweb, fastening on the solid white mass at its core.

"I seek the widow of the web!" His voice echoed through the silken chamber. A faint scuttling sound made him retreat a couple of steps. It stopped and he resumed his approach. A pair of pale cables quivered, then stilled.

As soon as the last echo of his cry vanished into the far reaches of the cavern, he was gifted with a stark reply: "Enter here and die!"

That was hardly encouraging, but then he had no reason to expect anything else. "I call the widow of the web!"

This time no response was forthcoming. He would have to force an audience. Carefully he chose the driest-looking cables and started out across them, aiming for the silken mass at the center of the web. It was hard to balance on the two unsteady cables and his physical skills were not what they used to be.

He was halfway across the web when a cable off to his left twitched. It was not connected to the ones he was slowly and patiently traversing. He forced himself to look up and across the web.

There it was: the white death. Drawn by his movements, the crystal spider had emerged from its ceiling hidey-hole, anxious to see what might have stumbled into its lair. It was bigger than a cow and transparent as old glass. The apparition would have shocked a normal man into insensibility.

Ynyr was sufficiently startled to lose his balance. He tumbled backward, flailing at the silk. This action only excited the crystalline arachnid. It moved rapidly now, turning toward the disturbance in the web, flashing glassy palps and dripping clear poison from fangs of dark diamond.

"Lyssa!" Ynyr shouted. No time left for subtlty or surprise. His fate would be decided in a few seconds. Even as he called out to her he was fumbling for the dagger at his waist. The spider's poison would paralyze without killing. He did not want to die slowly, sucked dry like an orange.

"Lyssa!"

The voice that had replied to his own when he'd first entered had been sharp and forceful. Now uncertainty bred hesitation. "Who speaks that name? Answer me!"

"It is Ynyr!" The spider was close now, nightmarishly close. No man should have to bear such a sight nor anticipate such a death. Far better to perish beneath the hooves of the Slayers' mounts or by one's own hand. He hefted the dagger, positioned it over his heart.

The voice came again. "I give you the sand in the hourglass."

The words he'd prayed for. The spider stopped, frozen by the movement of sand in the widow's strange glass. It would remain motionless until the sand ran out. Ynyr didn't know how much time had been given to him. He wasn't sure he wanted to know. Instead, he concentrated on making his way as rapidly as possible over the unsteady cables toward the mass of silk suspended at the center of the web.

The silk clutched and tugged at his body and limbs as if conscious of his presence, trying to hold him back until its spinner's spell was ended. He slashed at the cables with his arms, forcing a path where none existed. One wave of a groping hand uncovered a globular white mass. The skull showed two widely spaced punctures, one above each earhole. Ynyr knocked it aside and it went tumbling down through the web. A faint, final crash indicated how far it was to the rock below.

The sticky silk gave way reluctantly, but he adroitly avoided the worst spots, keeping to the dry cables the spider used itself. The central cocoon was close now.

Then he slipped. He'd rushed his approach. As he fell, he grabbed frantically for an overhead strand. It was thinner than the cables he'd been traversing, but it held long enough to enable him to swing into a net of thin webbing just beneath the cocoon. At the same time the spider seemed to regain its composure as well as its senses. It lunged across the gap, landing in the webbing just below the white sphere. But by then Ynyr had started to pull himself up into the cocoon.

The spider turned a slow circle, moving in short, erratic starts, pulling on various cables in an attempt to relocate the prey that had so mysteriously vanished. It rested there, sensing in its dull fashion that its supper was out of sight as well as out of reach.

Gasping for breath, not daring to glance back, Ynyr finally pulled himself up into the cocoon. The surface he relaxed against was unimaginably soft. He lay there a long moment before rising, then stood and inspected his surroundings. He likened the sensation to walking on a feather mattress ten feet thick.

The light that illuminated the cave was slightly brighter

here, as though it emanated from the silk itself. There were chairs, a mirror, other implements of human design. A bed of spun silk lay off in one corner. There was no suggestion of wood in its frame. It appeared to have been woven rather than built. He smelled freshly cooked food and his mind told him not to inquire into the nature of the ingredients.

Across the room sat a table. Various utensils decorated the top. Some were familiar to him, others not. A large hourglass squatted on the far side of the table. The old woman who sat there staring at him rested one hand atop the device. All the sand had collected in the bottom of the glass.

She didn't smile as she studied him. A finger tapped the side of the glass, marking thoughts as well as time. "I gave you the sand. You nearly used it all."

"I am not as sprightly as I once was and this body works not as well as the one I remember."

"None of us is young anymore."

He walked toward her. "Lyssa." Yes, it was she who shared name and more with the young woman betrothed to Colwyn. Age could not hide the resemblance.

What must she think of my appearance, he thought? Have I changed that much? From her stare he felt certain that he had.

None of us sees ourself true, he mused. It lies only in the power of others to do that. But I can see the past as well as the present in her eyes. She *remembers*. Whether that is good or ill we will soon know.

"I was young when I last heard that name."

He moved nearer, took a chair across the table from her. "I was young when last I spoke it to you."

"My face was as beautiful as my name then."

"More beautiful. You were renowned throughout the Fifty Kingdoms and men came even from across the seas to court you."

"None of them was suitable. Many were handsome, all

were wealthy, others brave and valorous. But none was suitable. Only you were suitable, Ynyr, and you would not stay with me.''

He did not turn away. This was not the time for turning away. But the memory was still painful. Let her take some solace from my pain, he thought. I too have suffered. Loneliness is a poor companion.

''I could not. You know that, Lyssa. There were many responsibilities, duties.''

''Ambition,'' she said tightly.

''It had nothing to do with ambition. Perhaps I was too forceful at times in expressing my hopes for the future. Some might interpret that as ambition. But for myself I wished nothing.'' He smiled gently. ''And as you can see by my appearance, that is precisely what I have gained. There were more important things to attend to. The fate of Krull was placed in my hands.''

''Ambition,'' she reiterated stubbornly.

''Is it ambition that one should wish to see Krull restored to its rightful place? Is it ambition that makes me sorrow as I watch the Slayers ravage quiet towns and villages and murder for pleasure? Is it ambition that I should want to see men rule their own lives and determine their own destinies instead of leaving them to the whims of the Beast?''

''You make it sound so noble,'' she murmured. ''So inevitable. As if you never had a choice.'' Her eyes flashed and beneath the age and the exhaustion and the bitterness there was a hint of the woman who had been. ''You *had* a choice. Every man has a choice. As for me, I grew tired of waiting. I despaired of you, Ynyr.''

''Great things can come to pass only if one exercises patience and caution.''

''Love does not make room for patience and caution. It burns wild for an instant and if not captured, it dies.''

"Do you think I don't know that? Do you think that while dreaming all my dreams and planning all my plans, I didn't think of that? Of you? My life has been as lonely as yours. Knowledge is little comfort on a cold night. I have lived a life as solitary as your own, without wife or children. You see, Lyssa, though I encountered many women from many lands who came to learn from me, you and I were too much alike. None of them was"—his smile twisted—"suitable."

She turned away from him. "You were not as alone as you believe. You had a son."

Here was the thing he'd feared most, the thing he had not prepared for, could not prepare for. No wonder her greeting had been so much harsher than he'd anticipated.

"You said nothing. You told me nothing. You let me leave in ignorance."

"I would not use such a thing to place a hold on you, Ynyr. There is no place in true love for such manipulation. I was alone when you left. I was alone!" She gestured weakly toward the woven bed.

"I killed him."

"You killed our son?"

"I killed him at birth. I was angry, mad with anger at you and what you'd done to me. I could not strike at you, so I struck at him. With him went the last vestige of my hope and my humanity." She gestured at the silken prison that enclosed them. "I know you cannot forgive me.

"This small room is my life now, my life and my punishment, and the web-spinner is my jailer. I am left only with wisdom I cannot use. Men come in hopes of stealing it. They leave the mouth of the cave in terror. Those who try to enter never leave at all."

She bent over the table. For the first time in many years, she cried, though whether the tears were for herself, for her slain son, or for what might have been, Ynyr could not say.

He reached out to her, touched her gently.

"I cannot forgive myself. I have already forgiven you. I did what I felt had to be done . . . but if I'd known it would cause you this life of pain . . ."

"It matters not. You cannot forgive a woman who has killed your son."

There was a small mirror nearby. The effort cost Ynyr some of his remaining strength, but he could feel the surge of love rising from deep within, reaching out to her.

"If I had not already forgiven you, Lyssa, how could I see you now as you were then?"

She changed as he stared, the wrinkles fading, the old Lyssa brought back momentarily through the power of love.

She looked at the glass, wiping at her eyes, and marveled at the image of the exquisite woman that lived for an instant in the shifting silica.

"You allow me to see back through time through your eyes. I had almost forgotten. I *was* beautiful, wasn't I?"

"Beyond compare." He fought to keep his emotions in check while holding the projection. "How could I have left you! Perhaps I deceived myself, perhaps I was afraid." The effort was too much. The mirror image rippled, became a true reflection of the woman gazing into its depths.

She reached across the table and for the first time her tone was comforting. "Poor Ynyr. You have suffered too, haven't you? You told the truth in that."

"I always told you the truth, Lyssa."

"And I would not let myself believe that anything could be more important than our lives together. Blindness and ambition. Fate has not been kind to us." She nodded at the mirror. "Your vision was a gift to me. I know what it has cost you and I thank you for it. My memory weakens with age. I too had forgotten much."

"Your vision can be a gift to me, Lyssa. You are the finest seer Krull has ever produced."

"That is why so many continue to seek me despite the depradations of my guardian, and why they would make use of my talent against my wishes."

"It is that and more that I seek to prevent, for there is another of power who is to be used against her will."

From anger to sorrow the widow's emotions changed to curiosity. "What can I see for you, Ynyr?"

"I need to know where the Black Fortress will rise tomorrow."

"Useless, dangerous knowledge."

"I need to know."

For a terrible instant he thought her old anger would overcome her again, but her voice stayed calm, her expression benign. "No. Time enough to dwell on half-forgotten dreams. Perhaps it is time for all dreams and furies to end. You still hope to work something against the Beast?" He nodded and she shook her head sadly.

"Poor Ynyr. Always the hopeful dreamer."

"Then leave me this dream to follow to its end, Lyssa. Help me. Help me to help the girl. She has been carried off and awaits the attentions of the Beast. You know what that would mean. The location of the Black Fortress on the morrow?"

She sighed. "How well I remember that relentless sense of purpose. I was a weak diversion for you at best, Ynyr. You are a fanatic when it comes to the pursuit of knowledge. Perhaps your cause is worthy, but I doubt it.

"Still, I will tell you what you wish to know. Your Fortress will materialize in the Iron Desert. But the knowledge is useless to you and those who travel with you, for you cannot leave here to impart it to them. Many have come, a few have entered, but no man has escaped the web."

"Somehow I must do so. The young girl I refer to who is being held in the Fortress has your name. There is much else of you in her.'' He recited a genealogy he knew she could not ignore.

"You lie!'' She rose from her chair and backed away from him, staring wide-eyed.

He walked slowly around the table and gently caressed a withered cheek. "Could I lie to you? I tell the truth now, as always. A young man seeks her. A young man the same age I was when you and I met. When you and I loved. He has much of me in him, though he knows not where it came from. In these two lovers all the planning comes to fruition, Lyssa. The Beast suspects and has drawn one of them into his lair. For there to be any chance of success in this matter her man must reach her before she is corrupted by the Beast. That is her last chance, and his—and Krull's. Help me, Lyssa. Help me to help them.''

Still stunned by his words and what they implied she turned away from him. "Would that I might, but what you require is beyond my power.''

Ynyr glanced at the hourglass. Of itself it was nothing: a transparent figure-eight filled with fine sand. What it stood for was everything.

Lyssa followed his gaze. "It may be turned only once. That is the law of the web.'' Her hand went to her forehead. "It would take a year before I could turn it safely again. I do not possess the resources to turn it twice in the same night.''

"Then there is nothing more to be done, is there? The other Lyssa will suffer our fate. She will grow old alone, in a place of darkness. If she is that fortunate. I shudder at the Beast's ultimate intentions.

"Nor will she live alone in her suffering. This whole world will become a place of darkness, of figures scurrying about in holes in the rocks, like your many-legged jailer. It will not be a world of men but of frightened, furitive creatures unable to face the light of day. Krull will enter a long night of fear and savagery."

Lyssa let the resultant silence fill the silken chamber. Then she turned to pick up the hourglass.

"These are the sands of my life, not of Krull's. If you carry them with you, the spider will have no power to harm you, but your own life will run out with the sand, for I will have to draw upon it as well as my own."

"I promised my life to this cause. I have no fear of sacrificing it now. But what of your life? You've made no such promise."

She did not meet his eyes. "I am tired, Ynyr. Seeing you again has made me realize how tired I really am."

"I'm sorry. That was not my purpose in coming to you."

She smiled gently. "I know that. As for my life, such as remains of it, I give it freely to the girl who bears my name and perhaps a little more of me than that, if all that you tell me is truth."

"It would be simple to lie now, and in good cause. But I cannot. I have told nothing but the truth since I set eyes on you, Lyssa."

Before he could move to intervene she slammed the hourglass against the table's edge. It broke like an egg.

Ynyr eyed the shattered instrument uncertainly, backing away. "I have said that I would give my own life, but I cannot take yours."

"It is too late, Ynyr. The decision is done. Already I have set in motion the restraints that will hold back the spider."

"No." He continued to back away from her. This was not how he'd wanted it to turn out. "I cannot take it."

"You must. By your own words, you must. You are hung by your own logic, Ynyr, and not for the first time. It is proper that our passing be presided over by such irony. We did not live long together, but if there is another life I will find you there.

"As for the girl, for all your confident talk I do not see how she and any man can prevail against the Beast, but at least if she is rescued she may live the life I lost long ago." She held out a double handful of sand to him.

"Hurry now, or this too will be wasted." Her face showed the strain she was under.

"For the life we lost." Ynyr approached and took the sand from her. He clenched his fist tight around the warm grains, a symbolic gesture of union. The sand, like their lives, began to trickle out through his fingers.

His hand went to his head but did nothing to alleviate the pounding that had begun there. Lyssa was hard at work.

"I cannot stop the sand," he told her.

"You can't stop time, Ynyr. I know. I've tried." She closed her eyes as if in sudden pain, felt for a chair and sat down heavily. Her face was flushed with the effort she was making and a vein throbbed in her neck. "Go now, while there is still time. Save the other Lyssa."

He backed out of the cocoon and as he did so it seemed that his last sight of the chamber was not of an old woman slumped over a table but of a lithe, delicate young girl. Then he wrenched his gaze away and started out across the web.

The spider was there, waiting for him, but confused and uncertain. It moved toward him and Ynyr held up his clenched fist, as though the sight of the sand itself would turn the monster. Whether it was the sand or something unseen, the spider suddenly halted, once again frozen in place by an unseen power.

He hurried down the sticky cables, his progress impeded by the sand he clutched tightly in his right hand. He would have cast it aside save that it was all that remained to him of Lyssa.

Even so, some of it fell from his fingers with each step he took, jostled as he was by the awkward descent.

Only when he'd reached the entrance to the cave did he pause to look back. The spider had gone berserk. It ripped and tore at the laboriously constructed web, the peculiar bond that had held it in check now abruptly broken. The cocoon did not survive the rampage. When it fell beneath the spider's onslaught, Ynyr's eyes dropped to the sand that slipped steadily through his fingers.

No time now for recriminations or regrets, he told himself firmly. No time to lament what might have been or to wonder if another path might have been the better one. Little time left now for anything. He staggered out of the cave, putting memories and the sounds of destruction behind him. The pain in his head had grown much worse. He knew he had to reach Colwyn before the sand ran out. It was a marker, a guide, a timekeeper. Something was slipping from him, something Lyssa had been forced to make use of.

United at last, he thought calmly. We were not strong enough, Lyssa and I. The Beast never feared us. But it fears Colwyn and Lyssa.

That thought gave him a burst of energy, helped to drive him wildly down the rocky path toward the giant forest at the base of the mountain. Lyssa and Ynyr were not to be.

Colwyn and Lyssa *must* be!

X

Colwyn stood by the same tree, staring at the flank of the mountain. It was very late or very early, depending on how a man chose to reckon time, and he was growing sleepy despite his resolve to remain alert. A few snores reached him from the direction of the encampment, Torquil's sharp basso rising above them all.

He turned and rubbed at his eyes. As he opened them again, he was surprised to see the young woman . . . Merith's assistant, she was—yes, that was right—still seated nearby, eyeing him closely. As soon as she noticed his eyes on her, she looked away and down.

"You don't sleep."

"No, I don't sleep, Colwyn. They all told me that I should call you Colwyn and not sire."

He smiled. "I prefer it that way. Titles make me nervous. A title has no personality. There's nothing to it save a thread to an uncertain past. I'd far rather be considered a man than a title. I've always considered them suitable for those who have no confidence in their real names and need something artificial to substitute for their real selves."

"I'm not sure I understand."

He remembered whom he was talking with. "It doesn't matter." He saw that she was working to hide her face from him and he moved nearer. "What troubles you?"

"Nothing troubles me, si—Colwyn."

"Your mouth says one thing, the rest of your face another. Tell me."

She looked up reluctantly, her voice subdued. "I was betrothed to a young man from my village. We were to be married this summer. But he traveled across the sea and his ship was lost. They say he drowned with the rest of his crew, but I don't believe it. I know he is alive. I know he will come back to me."

Colwyn rested a comforting hand on her shoulder. It was warm, softer than he expected. Perhaps she was not as bony as she looked.

"That's a good way to think. Always think positively, my father told me. It helps the digestion if nothing else."

Her hand reached up to touch his, the fingers moving slowly, gently. "It's hard being far from the one you love, not knowing if you'll ever see him again."

"Yes, it is hard."

She faced him squarely. "Some say that I shall be alone forever if my betrothed does not return."

"I'm sure that's not so."

"Merith keeps me working the cook-fires and the garbage to keep me from looking pretty."

"She's a good woman, but in that, at least, I think it's plain for anyone to see that she's failed."

"Perhaps my betrothed is not lost but has fled from the sight of me. All the village girls tease me about it."

"Then they are equally blind."

"You think it, too, don't you?"

"No, I don't think that, Vella."

He watched as the hood of her cloak was pushed back from her face. Somehow she'd avoided contact with the soot from the cook-fire. Her hair tumbled bright and lustrous about her face. Her beauty put Merith to shame.

Her attitude seemed to change. In place of the demure, shy servant girl there suddenly stood before him a confident young seductress. The moonlight drifting down through the trees gave her face an exotic cast.

When she spoke again, her voice was full of new confidence. Confidence, and something else: barely concealed desire.

"Tell me truthfully. Am I not worth returning to?"

Colwyn's eyes moved from hers and he cleared his throat, which was suddenly tight. He tried to think of other matters: of Ynyr on his mountain and what ordeals he might be undergoing; of Lyssa in her distant prison and what must await her. He did this because the longer he looked at her standing supple and anxious there beside him, the harder it became to think of anything else.

He'd been a long time alone. There had been the furious ride from Turold to Eirig, the tension attending the ultimately inconclusive wedding ceremony, the battle at the White Castle and Lyssa's abduction, and all that had subsequently befallen him since he'd set out to rescue her.

But Lyssa was far from this wood, and he was very tired.

Where the devil was Ynyr?

He found his gaze turning back to the beautiful peasant girl. Suddenly even Ynyr seemed very far away. . . .

*   *   *

The light was inconstant and deceiving, the twists and turns in the corridors endless. Lyssa ran onward, refusing to give up, the voice of the Beast booming and echoing all around her.

Abruptly she emerged into a wide hall lit with a milky glow. The walls here were higher than many she'd passed between during her long, seemingly endless run. The light itself seemed to twist and bend as she stared, forming eerie shadows and discomfiting silhouettes on the ceiling and floor.

Ahead lay a dome of some partly translucent material, ribbed with opaque, toothlike projections. It sat by itself in the center of the high-roofed chamber. It was made of material that differed from the rest of the Fortress.

She moved forward until she stood next to it, then searched for the safest passage around. There was movement behind her and she saw another of the silent white Slayers. A gap opened in the side of the dome. For an instant she hesitated, but no Slayers emerged from the gap. The path ahead was clear.

The walls of the passageway were contorted and warped according to some alien geometry. To see them was enough to know they hadn't been designed with human aesthetics in mind. She longed for the comforting, straight walls and angles of the White Castle.

She wondered at the sudden appearance of the passageway. Perhaps she'd tripped some concealed switch. In any case, there was the threat of the Slayers urging her onward. She ran forward.

The passage was not a long one and it instantly sealed itself behind her. She found herself standing in a dimly lit chamber. It took a moment for her eyes to adjust.

The sealing of the passageway behind her was ominous, but she wasn't entirely disappointed. If she was shut in, others were shut out. The closing prevented the Slayers from reaching her. For the moment it seemed she was safe from them.

She studied the floor and ceiling, which were fashioned of the same smooth material as the walls. She ran a hand along one curving section, following the arc down to the floor, but could not find so much as a crack where the two joined.

The air in the room was much warmer than it had been in the corridors or her cell, bordering on the sultry. She moved along the wall, searching for an opening, a lever, anything that might signify an exit or a means for producing one. There was nothing.

Except . . . there, across the empty floor from where she stood, a darker shape outlined against the blackness. Another doorway, perhaps. She hesitated, then moved toward it. Nothing there. Maybe a little farther on . . .

She halted and found she was shivering from a sudden chill, which did not come from a cold breeze. Carefully she retraced her steps until she was pressed tightly against the warm wall that had admitted her. She could retreat no farther.

At first it was only a sound—a faint, brushing sound like leaves scudding along a carpet. The sound was not distinct like footsteps, but more like a continuous rush across the floor, like something being dragged. A scratchy, rustling noise, not comforting to hear in near darkness.

Then something else—a steady pounding, deep and reverberant. It reminded her of the beating of her own heart, though whether this was the pulsing of another heart she could not have said, save that it was slower than her own and seemed to vary greatly in speed and intensity. With each pulse a brief flash of light temporarily illuminated a portion of the floor. She could not see the source of the light or tell if it was connected to the beating noise, but each time it flared to life she thought she could see something standing in the far portal she had considered entering.

Her fingers dug at the smooth wall. It helped to keep her from shaking so much. The thing that stood in the portal was very tall. In shape it was roughly human, but that was all that was human about it. She could not even tell if it was clothed or naked. She did not want to be able to tell.

Only the eyes showed clearly. They were enormous—oval instead of round—with bright red, vertically slitted irises. They focused on her where she stood frozen against the wall. At least, she thought weakly, there are only two of them.

She knew what it was without being told. Tales had been handed down through generations, old stories filled with more fancy than fact. Tales used to frighten unruly children. As a little girl she'd listened wide-eyed and trembling to such stories. She was not a little girl now. It would do no good to behave like one.

With a great effort of will she forced herself to stand away from the wall and regard the apparition as stolidly as it regarded her.

"Are . . . are you the Beast?"

"You may call me that if it pleases you. My own name for myself you would find difficult to pronounce, though it may be that in time you will come to know it."

"What do you want with me? The same thing that you want with the rest of my world?"

"No. If it had been my intention to destroy you, I could have done so long before now. You have been brought here not to perish before me but to give what you alone can give. You have been brought here for a marriage, though not of the sort you can imagine. It will be a much more intimate melding than you can conceive of."

"I don't know what you mean by such words but I do know this: if you could force this marriage or melding or whatever you choose to call it on me, you'd have done so when I was first brought here. But you've waited. Something has made you hesitate. So I think that perhaps you cannot take what you wish from me without my agreement.''

''You are hopeful rather than certain. For now it amuses me to leave you wondering. What I wish from you is a part of your mind, your soul. You are special, Lyssa of Eirig. Unique. In you many generations have combined to produce something atypical to your world. I would make use of it. It raises you far above the mass of insects you call your 'people.' Now, with my help and instruction, you will rise beyond your wildest dreams.''

''My dreams are not wild and I do not care to rise above them. As for help and instruction, I have already chosen a consort to share my life with me.''

Laughter seemed beyond the creature. ''You have chosen a paltry kingdom on an insignificant planet. I do not blame you for this. It is all you know. But there is more to the universe, much more. Why have a kingdom when you could rule an entire world? You could be queen and satrap in one, ruling absolutely.''

''I have no desire to rule at all, absolutely or otherwise. I have chosen love.''

''Love is fleeting,'' the Beast replied. ''An abstract notion that humans have clung to for far too long. It cripples you, makes you susceptible to the manipulations of others. Only power is eternal. You must learn to rise above such childish notions. You must grow.''

''One who rises beyond love has no soul.''

''One who has power need not worry about such superstitious nonsense.''

A clawed hand sprang to light in the darkness. As Lyssa stared, it became a ball of flame and leaped at her. She closed her eyes, expecting death. Instead, she found herself witness to a graphic demonstration of the Beast's power.

The flame slammed into the wall behind her, cracking and

scorching the material while leaving her cool and untouched. It backed off the wall and enveloped her for a bright orange instant before she felt herself rising in the chill flame's grip. It held her suspended for a moment, then set her down as gently as it had picked her up, and finally shrank to become a tiny, intense globe of drifting energy.

The fireball crawled up her leg, across her side and arm, and as she stared at it curling and rippling in her palm, became a freshly opened rose, its petals damp with dew. Behind her the wall smoked and gave off strange thick smells.

"Such is my power," the Beast rumbled, its voice echoing around the chamber. "It can be yours. What are infantile notions of love compared to this? You can command an army of men to do your bidding. All you have to do is desire it."

"I already command an army of men."

There was the fleeting image of a great arm moving through an arc in the darkness. "I see no army."

"Set me free and you shall see such an army as Krull has not seen in a hundred years."

"Ah, that I will not do. Consider, Lyssa. I offer you power far greater than any you can imagine."

"I don't want your power. I don't want anything that is a part of you, anything you have touched, anything you have made. I want nothing to do with anything that has your hand in it."

"Is it my form that frightens you? Is that what keeps you so set against the sharing I offer? That is easily remedied."

As she watched, the great reptilian eyes blurred, seemed to drop nearer the floor. The pupils became rounded, as did the eyes themselves. They advanced toward her. Soon they were near enough for her to see that they looked out at her from Colwyn's face, and she could not repress a gasp. Save for the red that shone deep within, she could not tell that the eyes regarding her were not Colwyn's.

"I can assume any form I wish. Whatever pleases you I can become. It is an art my people have practiced for a long time. Think. Any form at all. If you would prefer a cat or a watchful dog, I can become those as easily. Any form you wish, Lyssa of Eirig."

"What about an ant? Could you become an ant?"

"I am no infant. Do not think to toy with me. I can punish as well as reward. I would expect you to choose this form."

"There is no love in that form. There is nothing you can become that will hide what you are. There is no love in one who murders and destroys for pleasure."

"I do not deny that the activities of my Slayers provide me with amusement, but you are wrong if you think there is no more to it than that. There is purpose as well." The voice remained that of the Beast, for all that it issued from Colwyn's mouth.

"You still think love better than power? You think there is love in your boy-king? You are as naive as any of your people. Behold."

The figure turned and gestured at the wall. It split, to reveal night and tall trees instead of the glowing corridor outside the chamber. As she watched, it seemed that they moved closer, until she was standing just to one side of a towering forest giant.

Figures stood there, one that she recognized instantly. Colwyn was leaning back against the shaggy bark. She had no doubt that it was the real Colwyn, her Colwyn, and not some false image conjured up by the Beast to deceive her.

But who was the lithe young woman who clung so tightly to him, and whose embrace he did not reject?

She whirled to confront the Beast. "It's a lie! You say you can assume any form. I have heard of how you manipulate faces and bodies as easily as a sculptor plays with clay. Why should I believe that that"—she gestured at the image before them—"is any more real than the form you cling to now? You are as full of lies as a solicitor. You think to fool me with clever prevarication, but I am not so easily swayed."

"Indeed you are not, for you refuse the evidence of your own eyes. These walls do not lie. I have no reason to deceive you now, not when the truth works for me. Your Colwyn will betray you."

"He will not!"

"Then he will die," said the Beast calmly. "Either way, you will be rid of this silly, immature human infatuation. It will simplify your future."

Lyssa turned back to the image, unable to tear her eyes from it. Go away, she shouted silently! Vanish, disappear! I don't want to look upon you. But the image did not vanish, and she continued to stare at it.

The woman in Colwyn's arms was crying. Lyssa noted out of the corner of an eye that the Beast seemed to be observing the scene with equal interest. Even as she stared, the pale blue of the woman's eyes turned to black. Lyssa would have screamed save that she knew her warning cry would go unheard. Black eyes—as black as those of the Slayers, nearly as black as those of the Beast. The woman was something other than she appeared, and Lyssa had no way of alerting Colwyn.

Vella clasped the man tightly against her. She could sense that he was wavering, but still he resisted. "I have not held a man in my arms since my lover was swallowed up by the sea. It is good. You are a strong man, Colwyn. Lend me some of that strength."

"I know how painful it is to be far from the one you love," he murmured uncomfortably. "We share a common pain."

"Then, comfort me for one night, and let me comfort you. Share your strength with me, Colwyn. Have pity on me."

"Would that I might, but I can't betray my bride."

"One night is no betrayal. None need know what transpires in this place. I have listened to your men talk, and they say you are not truly married yet."

"It is true the ceremony was not finished."

"Then how can you speak of a betrayal?"

Colwyn's hand moved to touch first his chest, then his forehead. "Betrayal is more than a word. It is a thing that lies *here* and *here*. Not in the loins. I could comfort you as you desire, but you are wrong when you say none would know of it. *I* would know. That would be betrayal enough. I feel sorrow and sympathy for you, but I do not put aside a great trust so easily. Nor love. I can't take comfort with you when my true love has none."

"You will not, then?"

"Vella, in another time, another place, another existence, I would gladly lie with you. But that would be a different Colwyn, and you would be a different Vella. I cannot."

"Truly, I would be a different Vella," she whispered. Her right hand was behind him. It blurred, distorting. The fingers extended and the soft flesh turned to a horn-tough, scaly substance.

Lyssa could not stifle the useless scream in her throat, but Colwyn could not hear her as the claw rose toward his neck.

It stopped there, hesitating. "My master told me," Vella muttered with difficulty, as though talking to herself unwillingly, "make him betray her. If he will not, kill him."

Colwyn frowned down at her, his eyes telling him one thing, his ears another. But he'd already learned that where possible manifestations of the Beast were concerned, it was best to trust nothing, least of all one's own senses. He jumped away from her, his hand reaching toward the dagger at his belt, ready to cry out and alert his companions.

Yet still, sweet little Vella stood before him. Not even the inhuman claw she showed him changed that image, though his mind knew better.

"Yes," she said tightly, "*he* is my master. These talons were a heartbeat from your throat. I could have killed you in an instant."

"*Could* have." He did not draw the dagger, though his fingers hovered near the hilt. "You're still crying. Are those tears manifestations of the Beast as well as that claw?"

She wiped at her eyes and her voice was confused and angry. "They could be, but they are not. Nothing is as I was told it would be, nothing is as it seems. Uncertainty rules all. I long for the comfort of chaos." She smiled at him and her expression was distorted and torn. Her face seemed to blur as he looked at her.

"I am his creature that he fashioned too well. To tempt you he had to make me human, and in making me human his hold strayed. Now I am neither human nor his. I am a cruel joke, a pitiful jest." The smile broadened, giving her face a lopsided look. "I have had an hour of life, an hour of love, and this is better than all the days I have spent as his creature. That love is life for you but death for me. The last joke is on him, and that is best of all. I cannot comfort you, Colwyn, nor you me, but neither will he be comforted. Remember me."

In the Fortress Lyssa turned triumphantly to her jailer. "It is you who are betrayed, by a thing of your own making. Power is fleeting. *Love* is eternal. You cannot even control your own creature. Do not think to control me."

The Beast's only reaction was to wave a hand at the opening in the wall. The pulses of light from his body increased in frequency and intensity. The gap closed, shutting out the scene in the distant woods, but not before Lyssa had watched the unwoman Vella crumple and die. Poor thing, she thought. Neither human nor monster, but stuck somewhere pitifully in between. Better to die than live a pawn's life. She wondered if she'd have had the strength to make Vella's decision.

"Show me Colwyn again. Show me his reaction." There was no response from the Beast. Could it be that his powers to bring distant scenes near was limited? It must be, else Colwyn would have no chance to approach undetected. His lack of response encouraged her.

Then she was backing away as the false Colwyn shuddered and expanded. The red eyes bulged and rose. Once more the Beast confronted her in its true form.

"You are ignorant in the ways of power, Lyssa of Eirig. There is power such as shattered the wall behind you, power such as that which initiated and ended the brief existence of that slave—and then there is the power to withhold the use of power.

"Consider then *this* power. If you consent to join with me and be my human queen, I will halt all the attacks of the Slayers. It is in *your* power to stop the killing and burning. Each hour you delay, more people will die. Think hard on what I offer you. No more fields sent up in smoke, no more villages destroyed, no more children trampled underfoot. Delay and a little more of Krull perishes. Consent and guess how many more will live. An interesting game, is it not?

"Take all the time you wish. You cannot escape from here, nor can your lover save you, for he cannot even find this place. Relax and consider the number of deaths that can occur in an hour, in a day. You might even save his life, for at your consent I will call back all the Slayers.

"It is better, Lyssa, to exercise power than to abjure it. Better to be a god than a martyr. I leave you now to idle contemplation." The red eyes turned away from her. She could not see a far door open, could not hear one close behind her captor, but she sensed that she was alone once

again, sealed in the room that could be marriage chamber or
tomb, according to her own wishes.

She made certain he was gone before she buried her face in
her hands. Pressing her back against the wall, she slid slowly
down until she was sitting on the cool floor. She sobbed softly
and steadily.

Hurry, Colwyn, she thought. You've already proved him
wrong once this day. Now hurry and do so again, my love,
because this pain is too much for me to bear.

XI

Colwyn regarded the stain on the earth that had only a few moments earlier been the beautiful young woman he'd held so tenderly in his arms. There was nothing left to indicate that she'd ever been.

He knelt to touch the ground. It was already turning cold.

You were wrong, Vella, he thought to himself. You didn't die an inhabitant of some nether region between humankind and Beast-thing. You died as a woman. I would have been proud to have been your lover.

Vella's final scream had awakened Torquil. As he arrived to confront Colwyn, his eyes took in the stain on the ground, the absence of the peasant girl. He looked questioningly at his leader.

"She was something of *his*," Colwyn explained sadly, "but only until the end. She died Vella, a young woman of Merith's village. I would have her remembered that way."

Torquil's glance traveled down his friend's form. "She didn't harm you?"

"Only in my heart, and I forgive her for that. She only did her master's bidding." He raised his eyes to the trees towering overhead, half wishing that the Beast would appear before him in human form.

Torquil thought a moment. "Another changeling, like the one that took the place of the emerald seer."

"Yes, like the seer," Colwyn agreed, "only even more perfect, if such a thing is possible."

"Such magic must take a great effort, even for one as powerful as the Beast. She seemed as human as Merith."

"In some ways more human, I think."

Torquil studied the woods as if at any moment they might produce still another lethal deception. "He extends himself to produce something so perfect. I think maybe he's a little worried about you, Colwyn."

"Why?" He gestured at the earth. "Because I was able to survive this latest attack?"

"Because of that, yes. Believe it, Colwyn."

"Difficult to imagine, but a good thing to think of. I'd like to believe he's worried about us, yes. With luck we'll do more than worry him." He turned to glance back toward the mountain. "I wonder at Ynyr's absence. He should be back by now."

"How can we judge his needs? To penetrate the dangers of the web may require much time."

"Ynyr has little time left to spend, and less strength." He started toward the dark cliff that bulked sharply against the star-filled sky. "I'm going after him."

"He said that we were to wait here for his return."

"He also said that he'd be back soon. It is past soon. Stay and explain to the others."

"Is that the thanks I get for the help I've given you this far? I'm coming with you."

Colwyn glanced back, grinning. "I'd hoped you might."

"What, did you think I'd let you go on alone?"

"It had occurred to me."

"Well," the bandit leader said sheepishly as he lengthened his stride, "it had occurred to me too. Now we can forget about it."

Colwyn nodded, increased his pace to match Torquil's.

At the base of one of the forest giants, Titch lay sound asleep in the fragrant grass. The puppy that snuggled tight against him lay on its back, all four legs in the air. Every so often its nose twitched, as though checking the air for unfamiliar smells even as it slept.

Across the dying campfire Rell leaned on his trident, his single eye half-closed. Sensing movement, he looked toward the mountain. Two men stood close together, whispering. Together they turned and started toward the distant slope.

Rell straightened, stretched, and yawned as he considered the peaceful camp. Wisps of smoke rose aimlessly from the coals left behind by the fire. Wheezes and grunts came from sprawled, somnolent figures. He was part of this troupe and yet he was not. He made his own decisions.

Holding the trident at the ready he tiptoed through the sleepers and followed silently in the wake of the two who had departed.

The path down the mountainside was fit only for sharp-eyed goats and the darkness made matters worse. Ynyr staggered downward, his tired old eyes intent on the trail and the rocks that hid in wait to trip him. He knew that he must not fall. If he went down he was certain he would not be able to rise again. His breath came in long, painful gasps, each lungful the result of an agonizing battle his chest waged with the air. He gave silent thanks his course was all downhill.

Night creatures scampered clear of his legs or emerged from their hiding places to watch curiously as he stumbled onward. He could feel his strength leaving him even as the grains of sand trickled through his clenched fingers. He needed no such visual metaphors to know that precious little time remained. As she'd promised, Lyssa had drawn on his own reserves to keep the spider from him until he was clear of the cave. Those reserves could not be replaced. He was too old for rejuvenations.

How much farther could it be? He'd had the forest in sight for some time now, but mountain air and distances were ever deceiving, the more so on this night because of the size of the trees that formed the giant woods. He could feel the energy ebbing from his body. Despite the nearness of death he was calm. He'd been looking forward to greeting that old fakir for a long time.

But not until he'd imparted to Colwyn the vital information obtained at so high a price.

His legs felt rubbery and twice he nearly stumbled. I'm not going to make it, he thought sadly. Everything's been for naught: Lyssa's sacrifice, my own, the long journey from Eirig, all the old plans and hopes. But I *have* to make it. Colwyn's got to know.

Suddenly there were strong arms, young arms, supporting his own, easing his pale, trembling body to the ground. He blinked away the sweat, saw Colwyn standing over him staring anxiously down into his face. The thief Torquil stood nearby.

A good man, that Torquil, he mused. Strange how life forces both good men and bad into narrow corridors from which only extraordinary circumstances give them any opportunity to escape. If not for chance and accident, he and Torquil might have exchanged places in the scheme of things.

But not Colwyn. Colwyn's place had been carefully chosen.

He thought he detected a third figure lurking in the background but he couldn't be sure. It was growing darker by the minute. Even the stars were fading. He reached up and clutched Colwyn's jersey.

"At sunrise . . . at sunrise the Fortress will materialize in the Iron Desert. It will stay there until the following sunrise. You must reach it by then."

Colwyn looked to Torquil. The bandit leader was shaking his head sadly. Colwyn had studied his geography well, while Torquil had much practical knowledge of it. Both knew they could not possibly cover such a distance in a single day and night.

Ynyr's hand tightened, pulling Colwyn close. "You must reach it there or you will never find it again."

Gently Colwyn loosened the old man's fingers and tried to make him relax. "We'll reach it. Have no fear of that. And you'll be with us, to guide and counsel me."

Ynyr slowly shook his head. Everything was happening too quickly now. "No. My race is run." He twisted to gesture feebly at the weapon that hung from Colwyn's belt. "Remember all I have told you about the glaive. It does not make you invincible, but it is the second most powerful weapon remaining to the people of Krull. Use its power wisely. Do not squander it. When it is gone it cannot be restored."

"I've learned of power and its uses from you, Ynyr. I won't forget."

"And I've learned a little more of life from you. A hermit's existence facilitates study but the intensity of one's focus creates a narrow vision." He lifted his head slightly to look past Colwyn to Torquil. "You chose men I would not have chosen, but they were the right men.'' Torquil shifted uneasily at the compliment.

Ynyr's eyes locked with Colwyn's. ''There is much I should have told you, many things you deserve to know that I saw fit to withhold from you. Now you must learn them for yourself. The time of teaching is past.''

Frustration filled Colwyn's face. ''I don't understand.''

''You will. You *must*. Your marriage...'' He drew in a wheezing breath. ''Your marriage to Lyssa was necessary.''

''Of course it was. The alliance between Eirig and Turold—''

Ynyr was shaking his head. ''No, no! Truly you do not understand, for which you cannot be blamed. So much was kept from you. It was necessary that you mature and reach decisions uncontaminated by too much knowledge. The marriage... you must rescue Lyssa!''

''I know. Just rest now.''

''No,'' Ynyr said violently, ''you *don't know*! You don't know that... that...'' He hesitated, staring through Colwyn for a moment. Then his gaze dropped from Colwyn's face to his own right hand. There was a look of surprise on his face. He opened his fingers. When he spoke again, it was in the voice of a young man: ''The sand is gone.''

Colwyn looked. The night wind scattered the few remaining grains from the old man's palm. When he looked again into Ynyr's face, the wizened old eyes had closed for the last time.

He rose. There was no anger in him and less sorrow than he'd expected. Ynyr had chosen this moment, as surely as Colwyn had determined to marry Lyssa. He desperately wanted to know what the old man had been so frantic to impart before his passing. Now it seemed he would never know, unless...

''You must learn them for yourself,'' Ynyr had said.

Torquil put a comforting hand on his shoulder. "I understood very little of what he said, and I knew him not overlong, but for a wise man he seemed like a decent chap."

"He was the wisest of the wise," Colwyn muttered. "I wish he had not chosen this course. I will miss him."

"If you believe in his wisdom, then you won't stand here regretting its loss. You'll make use of it, as he instructed you to." He glanced back toward the camp. "I wish he'd been wise enough to tell us how we're supposed to get from here to the Iron Desert in a day and night."

"We'll get there." Colwyn's assurance was so palpable that Torquil elected not to argue the point further.

Instead he turned and started downhill. "Then we'd better wake the others and get started. I haven't made a long run in a year. I don't know how many of the others are in shape for such an attempt."

"First we bury him." Colwyn nodded toward the now peaceful form.

"We waste time, Colwyn."

"No time spent on Ynyr the Wise is wasted."

"Colwyn," Torquil said evenly, "Ynyr the Wise is dead."

"His spirit will travel with us. I want that spirit laid to rest in comfort. First we bury him."

Torquil sighed. "As you command."

Rell turned away from the sight. There was much he'd hoped to ask of the wise man. Now he would be denied that opportunity. That had always been his people's curse; failing to ask the right questions in time. Now there was only one opportunity left to him, and he had no intention of wasting it.

The cairn they raised above the grave was simple and devoid of decoration, as Ynyr would have wanted it. The old man had a horror of waste when he was alive.

Ergo spoke the words and for a change lived up to his sobriquet, the Magnificent. When he'd finished and the last

rock had been piled in place, Colwyn turned his attention to
Torquil.

"I did not mean to appear obstinate in this matter. Your
concern is justified, of course. Has he died in vain? The Iron
Desert is a thousand leagues away."

Torquil was certainly no optimist by nature, but neither was
he the kind of man to quietly accept defeat. "We'd better get
started. Perhaps we can somehow reach the place."

"No man can cover that distance in a night and a day,"
said Kegan. "Not the greatest runner on all Krull could do it,
and I am not he."

"Nor am I," added Colwyn, "but we are bound to try.
Perhaps we can find additional horses along the way."

"Not even a horse could make such a journey."

Rell stepped out of the brush, spoke quietly: "No normal
horse." All eyes turned to him. "But the fire-mares might do
it. They do not run in the manner of normal steeds."

"No, and they don't behave like normal steeds either,"
Torquil snapped. "No man has ever saddled a fire-mare."

"Someone must always be first. I have saddled and ridden
them. It can be done, though not for much more than a day.
Longer than that and you lose the strength to hold on."

"We would all have to have mounts," Torquil continued to
argue. "What you suggest is impossible."

"An impossible task confronts us; Rell proposes an impossible solution. I see no conflict there." Colwyn turned to the
cyclops. "I have heard stories that speak of such a herd living
to the south of here, near the place where the great plain
meets the foothills."

Rell nodded. "Your storytellers speak truth. There is time,
if we move quickly and prepare."

"Enough debate, then. Titch and Ergo will remain here
with Merith."

Ergo stepped forward. "They most certainly will not. I

have traveled a long way with you, Colwyn of Eirig, or Turold, or wherever you choose. Perhaps I haven't always lived up to the claims I've made for myself, and I am no seer when it comes to practicing the arcane arts, but I know a few things. That makes me valuable to a party of thickheads like this one." For once no one took him to task.

"You once said that I had courage. It hasn't deserted me." He looked around with an amazed expression on his homely face. "Am I really saying all this? By Krull, the man offers a chance to back out with honor and I'm actually arguing to go with him!" Laughter burst from the assembled thieves.

But when Ergo turned to face Colwyn again, his tone had grown serious. "It is not your decision to make, Colwyn. I've earned the right to go on with you to the end."

"The end may be death."

Ergo shrugged. "So be it. I've lived a short life but a full one." He grinned. "I have experienced the lord of all gooseberry trifles, have consumed the supreme dish. I claim the right to go from dessert to desert."

Colwyn nodded his approval. "How can I resist in the face of such brilliant oratory? I concede."

A small voice sounded from behind Ergo, and Colwyn could see the boy peeping out at him. "I want to come, too."

"No, Titch," Colwyn told him. "You're too young. Ergo may have lived a short life, but you've lived none at all. It would be wrong to throw away what you don't have."

"I haven't been in the way. If the seer was still alive," he hesitated, fighting back tears, "he'd say that I should go so that I could learn. Besides, Ergo told me that you were my family now." He looked around at them. "All of you."

"It's true that the boy has nowhere else to go," Ergo pointed out.

Colwyn considered, reluctantly gave in. "You're right

again. All right, Titch, you can come, but stay clear of trouble and mind what you're told."

"I will, sir," the boy said solemnly.

They hurried to break camp. Merith moved to embrace Kegan.

"I know that I can't make you come back to me only," she murmured, "but if you survive, I ask you to consider it. I'd make you as happy as any one woman could."

"Be damned if I don't think you're right about that," he admitted. "No promises, but I'll think on it."

She smiled and kissed him. "That's all I ask."

The journey was not long and the canyon itself a rainbow of breathtaking shapes and colors, but there was no time for sight-seeing.

Colwyn crawled to the edge of the cliff, stopping only when he could see clearly over the edge. They had no time to waste and there must be no mistakes. Everything had to work perfectly on the first attempt, Rell warned him, or they would have to think of another way to cover the distance between the plains and the Iron Desert. The herd would not give them a second chance.

The cyclops bellied up alongside him. Below lay a narrow canyon, its water-worn tributaries twisting and curving in the moonlight, a valley of sedimentary serpents.

"You must know," Rell whispered, "that they can leap any barrier. But they still think and react like any horses. The surprise and shock caused by our trap should make them react without thinking. That is our only ally. If we delay in taking them and give them time to consider their situation, they'll gallop straight out of this canyon despite anything we can do to block them."

"Everyone knows what he has to do," Colwyn replied.

"We'll work as fast as we can, but you're still the key to our success, Rell."

The cyclops nodded. "Don't worry about me."

"I don't plan to. Besides, that boy is probably doing enough worrying for all of us."

Rell looked wistful. "A good lad, little Titch, for a two-eye. I do not frighten him the way I do most human children."

"He hasn't had a usual childhood. When this is concluded I have to see that some is given to him." He would have said more but the cyclops forestalled him, raising a huge hand.

"Listen!"

A faint rumble from the far end of the canyon; a distant pounding coming closer, growing steadily louder. Hoofbeats they were, and yet somehow different, as though the wind itself fled before them. Court storytellers had often regaled the young Colwyn with fanciful, highly embroidered tales of the many wondrous creatures that roamed Krull's open plains, but being a sheltered youth he'd never had the chance to seek any out. Many times he'd sought assurance from his father that the storytellers were telling him the truth and not simply entertaining him with images drawn solely from their imaginations. His father had assured him they were not.

"The fire-mares are real, my son. As real as Turold, as real as you or I or this castle. What a cavalry we would have if they could be broken to the saddle! All our enemies would fall before us. But alas, no man has been able to master them."

Colwyn remembered as he studied the canyon and listened to the thunder rising from within.

"What must be done?" he asked Rell.

"The leader is the key. Once she is taken and saddled, the others will follow. Our trouble rises from the fact that this is no normal herd.

"There is little to distinguish between leader and followers. They are crafty and wise and have been known to play tricks on would-be captors, such as placing their true leader not at the herd's head but in the middle."

"Then how will you know her?"

"I will know. I told you once that there are times when one eye can see more clearly than two. This is such a time. Leave that to me and make certain the others are ready. The more noise they can make, the more confusion we can cause, the easier it will be for me to isolate the leader."

Then there was no more time for talk, for the objects of their search suddenly appeared in the canyon. Colwyn was struck speechless by their beauty. Independence glistened in their eyes while rippling flanks and pounding legs bespoke immense strength and endurance. In size they were larger than the largest horses he'd ever seen. Truly there was much power here, for those who could make use of it.

He stared intently into the milling herd as two men rode in behind them, shouting and hooting and cracking their whips, but he could not determine which among them was the leader. It was as confusing as Rell had promised.

Was it the black one with the white markings out there in front? But according to the cyclops, position within the herd meant nothing. There—that immense older mare trotting lightly in the second rank, the one with the golden tail! Or the mottled gray nuzzling her?

Then Rell's fingers were clutching his shoulder and he rose, cupping his hands to his mouth. "Down and at them!"

As the robbers plunged down among them, ready with ropes and saddles, the herd twisted about in disarray, searching for an exit. Oswyn threw his saddle over one mare's back so quickly that she couldn't avoid him, but both rider and saddle held their position only long enough for the mare to send both flying to the ground.

It was the same everywhere else. One man would get a noose around a powerful neck or a bridle over a bucking head for a few seconds before they were dislodged, or another would find himself riding a broad back one second and hard ground the next.

Confused and uncertain, the herd wheeled in uneven circles around the middle of the canyon. The men continued their spirited shouting, waving their arms and trying to back their quarry still farther up the steep slopes. But the delaying action could not work forever. Before long, the leader would determine that there was more noise than threat in all the activity. Then she would take to her heels and lead the escape in spite of anything mere men could do.

Even as the herd slowed and milled about, waiting for their leader to give them direction, Colwyn was whirling the rope and its heavy noose overhead. Patiently he kept it in motion as he sought to isolate the mare Rell had selected. If he'd guessed wrongly and she wasn't the herd leader, then all the carefully coordinated effort would be waste. He didn't dwell on the possibility.

He flung the loop. It soared cleanly between two bucking fire-mares to settle around a piebald neck. The mare whinnied loudly, loud enough so that her cry rose above the echoes of falling rocks and shouting men. She kicked and turned even as Rell grabbed hold of the rope, pulling both men flat and dragging them across the rough ground. Colwyn had the rope looped several times around his right arm. The mare might pull the arm out of its socket, but he was determined she would not separate it from the rope.

Gravel and sand pitted his skin and stung his eyes as she pulled them across the canyon floor, but he clung grimly to the rope, trying to get to his feet and dig in. Torquil tried to help but was too far behind to reach them.

All around the bandit leader, his men were being thrown

aside, and they were good riders, too. The cyclops was wrong. Mere men couldn't ride these cursed creatures! In his mind's eye he recalled the difficulties they'd already over-come to get this far. Now it seemed they were to be defeated for taking the word of a one-eye.

But even as he began to despair, Rell struggled to his feet. His weight and strength slowed the leader. Then Colwyn was on his feet next to him, fighting his way along the line toward the great beast. She snorted and reared angrily before him and he had to dodge hooves and teeth.

Rell slid sideways until he stood behind a rock firmly anchored to the earth. With his feet thus braced and muscles straining, he managed to keep the fire-mare under control.

"Hurry!" he urged Colwyn. "I will not break, but I can't vouch for the rope, and if she thinks to snap at it she may bite it through."

Colwyn kept the cyclops's warning in mind as he approached the bucking mare with saddle and bridle in hand. His eyes stayed on those flying hooves and he was mindful not to approach too quickly. The herd milled nervously around them, perhaps aware now of the way out of the trap, but unwilling to try it without direction from their leader.

"Easy, my beauty, stand easy," Colwyn murmured consolingly as he drew near. "Temper your impatience. A day's ride and then you'll be free again."

By the time he came alongside, she'd relaxed a little, winded by her fight with thepe. Rell kept it taut as Colwyn slipped onto the fire-mare's back. Then he was safely in place.

Making sure of his seat, he nodded to Rell. The cyclops let loose of the rope and backed clear as the mare immediately galloped off. The herd began to flank her, whinnying their concern.

For an instant Colwyn feared she'd bolt for the exit, but a

touch of his heels and a tug leftward on the reins changed her mind. By the time he directed her back toward his friends, he felt he had her fairly well under control. Still, he did not relax. It would be presumptuous to think he knew her. A flick of massive back muscles could still send him flying.

The longer he rode her, however, the less likely that seemed. She had turned into a model of equine decorum.

"Gentle as a baby," he said to Torquil, who watched him approach warily, ready to retreat if the mare charged. He eyed those pacing hooves uneasily.

"Some baby." He turned, shouted commands. "Saddle the others! Quickly!"

Some of the chosen fire-mares still resisted, but most did no more than canter nervously around their docile leader. They were not broken, but the fight had gone out of them. As long as their leader stood placidly in their midst, there seemed no more reason for alarm, not even when strange things like saddles and surcingles were placed on their backs.

As the last mounts were being chosen, Rell walked up to Colwyn. "I must remain here."

This was not expected. "Why? We'll need you when we assault the Fortress. You're worth any half dozen in a fight, Rell. Why withdraw your support now that—" He broke off, remembering what Ynyr had told him about the one-eyes and their bad bargain of ancient times.

"Forgive me, Rell. I've been so involved with my own problems that I tend to forget other men have their own. Is it time, then?"

Rell nodded somberly. "Before night falls again, my night will come for me."

Colwyn leaned down to grip the cyclops's shoulder. "You've done enough. More than enough. More than could be asked of any *man*. Stay here. In peace." He straightened in the saddle and looked around the canyon. "This is a quiet place.

A good place. None should disturb you here, not even
Slayers.''

"Each to his fate," Rell murmured, adding a gentle smile.

"Each to his fate. Yours to stay, mine to go on. If not for
Lyssa I'd be tempted to give up. But while she suffers, I
suffer.''

"Not to waste any more time, then," Rell advised him. He
nodded toward the open end of the canyon. "Your way is
clear, as is mine.''

Colwyn nodded, urged his mount toward the opening. The
others followed, still settling themselves on their strange but
willing mounts, talking steadily to them to show they meant
no harm. Torquil rode alongside Colwyn. As they passed
Rell, he glanced curiously from the unmounted cyclops to
Colwyn, who said nothing but explained all with a single,
eloquent shake of his head.

Rell turned and walked over to where Titch stood watching
Kegan secure his own mount. He came up behind the boy and
lifted him easily up behind the man. Titch turned to say
something, then caught the look in the cyclops's eye. Life
with the seer had made the boy perceptive as well as quiet. In
that single glance he saw what awaited his great friend, and
how near at hand it lay. For a boy he was very strong. There
were not many tears.

That single eye produced only one. Gently Rell backed
off.

Kegan watched curiously, said nothing until Rell had moved
away. "He's not coming with us?"

"It is his time to die," Titch said softly.

Kegan was a practical man, not a diplomat. "We'll miss
his help. If he's going to die anyway, why doesn't he come
with us?''

"No. He must stay here and accept his fate. If he opposes
it in any way, he will bring great pain on himself.''

Kegan shrugged, urged his fire-mare forward. "A strange way to live. A stranger way to die. Be thankful, boy, we were given two eyes instead of one."

Ergo rode last in line and was quick to note the exchange. He turned in his saddle. "Rell!"

"I must stay here, my magnificent friend. You and Titch have already realized your wishes. Soon I will realize mine."

Ergo reined his mount in. "We had no time to be friends. I mistrusted you when I first met you."

"And I was equally unsure of you," Rell replied.

"No time. Never enough time, it seems. I wish . . ." He shrugged helplessly. "Good-bye, *friend*."

"Farewell, Ergo. There was time enough for friendship. Go now without looking back. There'll be nothing to see."

But Ergo could not help looking back. Rell stood staring after the departing troupe, solid as the rock walls that enclosed him, until they swallowed him up.

Colwyn kept the pace easy until they were clear of the canyons. Ahead lay the southern plain and beyond, where the grass rusted, the Iron Desert. And Lyssa. Thoughts of her freshened his resolve. They had a long way to go.

Kicking his mount's flanks as hard as he could, he chucked the reins and let out a shout. The mare started, reared, then let herself go. The breeze in Colwyn's face became a gale, then a hurricane. Soon he was no longer riding, he was holding on for his life.

Behind him he heard yells and cries as his companions urged their steeds to keep pace. Hazarding a glance backward, he saw the frightened faces of his men hugging tight to massive necks, saw whitened fingers clutched convulsively around taut reins. Below the men were pounding, wondrous bodies, and between them and the earth were only blurs riding streaks of fire.

Carefully he sat up in the saddle and squinted into the

wind. At this pace they might indeed reach the Iron Desert in time.

It had been a slow week and the boatman was hungry for a little business. He scratched at himself as he emerged from his hut, tugging at his jacket and grumbling at the lateness of the hour. Now, what fools would come atraveling this time of morning, when the moon insisted it was still night, no matter what the clock might say?

Well, they'd pay and pay plenty for disturbing him at such an unholy hour. Automatically he looked to his right. His ferry bobbed lazily at anchor, ready for the next crossing.

"Oh, you'll pay dearly for this boatride, gentlemen, whoever you are. And if you're nobles you'll pay in gold or get yourselves wet!"

Odd. Beneath the rumble of approaching hooves he thought he detected a faint hissing sound, like a kettle boiling over on a stove. Distant lightning, perhaps. At least it sounded like a large party. The night should prove profitable. If he felt like it and they were desperate enough to cross, he might make them pay for the whole week.

Suddenly he was fully awake and his eyes bugged as he saw the fire coming toward him. He looked wildly from right to left and finally threw himself onto the riverbank, hardly daring to look up.

But there was no explosion of water from riders plunging into the river. He gaped upward as the horses, trailing flame from their hooves, cleared the river in a single awesome bound to land safe and dry on the far shore. In another instant they were gone.

"Was that a dream?" he mumbled aloud. Nay, it was as real as the mud caking his face and clothes. He picked at it as he sat up and stared across the river. Before long his earlier mood had returned. Not only had he lost his expected customers, now he would have to pay some old woman in the village to clean his working clothes.

"And I'd have settled for a little silver," he groused as he staggered back into his hut.

XII

Hearts pounded uneasily as the fire-mares drove their tireless way across the plains, particularly when they leaped a certain deep gorge no normal horse could have negotiated in three jumps. Confident and powerful they might be, but a man could only handle so much magic in one night. At least no one was in any danger of falling asleep in his saddle. Terror is a wonderful stimulant.

They'd reached the desert by the time the sun showed itself above the horizon. Red sand and gravel exploded beneath fiery hooves as the mares, seemingly as fresh as they'd been back in the canyon where they'd been saddled, thundered onward at Colwyn's urging. Strange green and brown plants appeared, causing those men with any strength to spare to wonder at their eerie shapes and absence of leaves.

Soon Colwyn was forced to slow. They were approaching a mountain. The mountain had regular sides and peculiar overhangs, and projections. In the rising suns it shone a dull black.

Torquil reined in beside him and Colwyn pointed with his right hand. "There it is. I'd not thought to see such a thing. When this day is done, maybe we'll never have to see it again."

The Black Fortress towered before them, rising windowless and cold from the desert floor. Beneath, the ground had been permanently altered. Now it would do the same to the lives of the men who sat staring at it.

"Yes, there it is," Torquil muttered as he gazed at the alien monolith, "and none but us madmen would want to get this close to it."

There was no mistaking the resolve in Colwyn's voice. Knowing that at last they sat in sight of Lyssa's prison had revitalized him.

"We're going to get a lot closer to it. Closer than even madmen dream of getting." He glanced at the sky. "And quickly. It's almost sunrise." He led the charge toward the Fortress.

They spread out, combing the slick surface, having trouble keeping their footing on the glassy substance. Colwyn couldn't help but admire the construction. It was as smooth as the blade of a good sword and showed little sign of wear.

"Solid rock," Torquil groused, "or solid something, anyway. Might as well be rock. Not even a crack where an ant could force an entry. And steep enough to give a mountain goat pause." He eyed Colwyn, his gaze dropping significantly to the glaive slung at the prince's belt. Colwyn noted the glance and his hand went to the weapon. For a moment he considered using it.

Then he loosened his grip and shook his head. "No, not yet. It's not the right time. Ynyr warned me not to waste its power."

"You'll have no chance to use it if we can't get inside."

"We'll get in," Colwyn assured him. "We haven't come

this far to be stopped at the last moment by the absence of a door.''

"How will we get in? Even if we can find a door, what makes you think it will open from the outside?"

"We *must* find a door." He looked upward at the towering walls that rose toward the rapidly lightening sky. "And soon."

"Colwyn, watch out!" Oswyn yelled.

Above, a gap had opened in the side of the Fortress. Colwyn ducked just in time to avoid a blast of energy from the spear of a white Slayer. Other bursts struck all around him. Torquil huddled behind a dark protrusion. If they could just get within ax range of the Slayer . . .

Then another portal opened where none existed a moment before, and still another. The Slayers would step into the opening and attack, then retreat to the safety of the Fortress's innards. On open ground the men would have charged, but here they could barely cling like lice to the steep side of the Fortress.

Colwyn leaned out, tried to locate the nearest opening. "We've got to get inside!" he muttered loudly. He waited until the Slayer stationed above had used his spear and withdrawn, then started upward.

But another appeared farther to the left and sent a stream of death toward Colwyn. He ducked, and lost his footing on the slick surface.

"Colwyn!" Torquil yelled. He reached out, and a blast of fire from above nearly severed his arm at the shoulder.

But a thick-fingered, powerful hand had Colwyn by the shirt, pulling him to safety. An instant later the stocky, slow-witted thief staggered as he took the full force of a Slayer's spear.

"Rhun!" Colwyn shouted. Quickly he pulled the wounded

man to shelter . . . too late. "Rhun. A foolish act for a man who thought this adventure useless."

The heavyset thief was breathing hard. He looked up at Colwyn, too stunned to feel the pain. "I was wrong. The journey was worthwhile. Finish it for me."

His eyes closed and there was no more hard breathing. Torquil had worked his way across to squat alongside. "A brave man, good fighter. A little slow up here"—he tapped his head—"a lot bigger down here." His fingers touched his chest.

Gently Colwyn set him aside, his teeth clenched in anger and frustration as he looked upward. "We can't sit here like this. We have to charge them."

Torquil shook his head. "They'll pick us off as soon as we stand. We have to keep to cover or we'll end up like Rhun."

"We've no choice." Colwyn pointed skyward. "Soon the Fortress will move. If we're trapped out here when that happens we'll probably die anyway."

Again Torquil's gaze fell to the glaive secured at Colwyn's belt. It wasn't time, Colwyn knew. It wasn't time. But they were running out of options. His hand dropped to the ancient weapon, felt of the cold metal, the power there.

"Wait," Torquil told him. He was looking out across the plain, back the way they'd come, away from the Fortress. "Look there."

A line of smoke and fire was coming toward them. Colwyn frowned. Slayers coming to trap them? He squinted in the still uncertain light. But it was Ergo who first made out the strange trident outlined against the Eastern horizon.

"Rell!" He stood up, nearly lost his thoughtless head to a Slayer spear.

"Stay down!" Colwyn ordered him. He sat and stared in wonder as the cyclops reined in at the base of the Fortress and began climbing toward them. The giant did not speak, did not pause, but continued climbing past the piniomed men, toward the first of the openings in the Fortress wall.

A burst from a spear struck him, then a second. He shook but never slowed, staggered slightly but did not loose his grip.

"He's shielding us," Torquil murmured, watching in admiration as the cyclops continued his relentless climb.

Colwyn stood. "Follow him! For your lives!"

Rell was at the entrance to the Fortress now. Another burst from a spear struck him even as he lowered the massive trident and charged forward. The nearest Slayer hardly had time to scream as it died a tri-pronged death.

There was a new sound, a slow ponderous rumbling from somewhere within. The entrance began to close around Rell. Arms the size of small trees shot sideways. Even Rell could not stop the walls from closing, but he slowed them, even as fresh Slayers appeared to strike him again and again.

Torquil and Kegan were the first to slip inside beneath those straining arms, and the two Slayers perished under their weapons. The others followed, with Colwyn the last inside.

But while the walls still stood far enough apart to admit a normal man, they had closed too tightly for Rell to escape. He stood straining, but his strength was at an end.

"Torquil!" Colwyn shouted. "Brace your ax in the opening!"

The thief tried, but the blade twisted and groaned against the walls. "No good . . . there isn't enough room to get the blade in sideways."

"No use," said Rell. "This is my time. Remember, Colwyn. Each to his fate."

The last of his strength vanished and as it did so, the walls closed in on him with a rush. Colwyn and Torquil backed away, staring, helpless.

Behind them the others were also watching, but Titch was the only one who spoke. "He opposed it, and he died in great pain, just as he said would happen. I wish I could be so brave.''

"So do we all," said Ergo, putting an arm around the boy. "But we're all not like Rell."

Fire exploded behind them and they rushed to deal with the fresh group of Slayers who appeared in the corridor beyond. There was no more time for regrets, nor would Rell have wanted them.

Ahead, the corridor suddenly opened into a vast chamber. Beyond lay a narrow bridge guarded by Slayers. Ignoring the abyss beneath, the men rushed onward. One caught a blast in the chest and died long before he reached the bottom of the chasm. But they cleared the far end of the bridge, only to find themselves slowing as they entered still another passageway. A few steps farther brought them to an intersection.

Torquil looked right, then left. The side corridor was indistinguishable from the one they were in.

"Which way? Both look alike to me."

Colwyn took a step forward. "Straight on, as we've been going."

"How do you know that's right?" Bardolph frowned at the juncture. "How can you tell direction in this place? There's nothing to judge by."

Colwyn didn't hesitate, stepped confidently forward. "I don't know how I know, but I *know*." He nodded ahead. "It's this way."

"Then perhaps we should go another way," Ergo put in, but his jest passed unappreciated. No one was in a very jocular mood.

Concentrating on the path ahead, none thought to check the small side recesses that pockmarked the tunnel. So no one saw the Slayer that stepped out of the darkness to heave a spear at Torquil's back. No one except Kegan, who moved fast while trying to shout a warning.

"Torquil! Look ou—!"

The spear took him in the side and the Slayer came after it. Oswyn cut him down, continuing to hack at the motionless body long after the life had fled from it.

Torquil bent over the wounded Kegan, inspecting the injury. Bitterly he saw there was no reason to remove the spear.

"That was stupid," he said through clenched teeth.

"I . . . I agree," Kegan said dully. "Looks like my traveling days are over, my friend." His back arched spasmodically, his eyes wide. "That hurts. A just end to a frivolous life, though I wish it had come outside under the clean sky. This is no place to be buried."

"Don't worry," Torquil muttered. "We'll get you out of here."

"Doesn't matter. Don't waste the time. Here's where I fell and I guess here's where I'll stay. Tell . . . tell Merith I loved her. Tell her she was my favorite. And tell Lona I loved her, and *she* was my favorite." He winced, then the old smile returned. "You understand."

Torquil nodded. "I understand."

A little sigh escaped Kegan's lips. "I did love them all, you know." A second sigh, then stillness.

"I know," Torquil said softly. Gently he passed a hand over the staring eyes, closing them. Better a good man should look inward for eternity than at the walls enclosing them.

Colwyn stood silently behind the bandit leader. It was not his place to comment.

Finally Torquil stood. His expression was grim, resolved. "He knew the risks and accepted them of his own free will. So do we. So do we all."

"A few must die so that many may live," said Oswyn. "The old man said that one night. I heard him, but I never thought I'd find myself agreeing with him."

"If we are those few . . ." Bardolph began.

"Then so be it," Ergo finished for him. Besides, he told himself resignedly, we are committed. But somehow the sarcasm rang hollow. A vague sense of purpose had driven them to accompany Colwyn on his quest. Now something powerful gripped them all, even he who'd never been one to volunteer for desperate causes. Kegan's death underlined what they'd already accomplished, as well as hinting at what they might yet achieve.

Glory and greatness are such abstracts, Ergo mused, until circumstances make them real.

"Lead on," Torquil told his king.

No more deadly surprises waited to greet them. No matter how brightly lit or inviting the intersecting corridors appeared, none swayed Colwyn from his chosen course.

So intent were they on the dangers that might assail them from the side or above, however, that no one noticed the hairline crack in the floor ahead.

It opened noisily and fast, the sound warning them barely in time. Whether their footsteps or an unseen hand had triggered it, none could say. Not that it mattered. The slick, rounded corridor sent them tumbling downward, scrambling for a handhold.

Torquil, Colwyn, and Bardolph barely managed to hold on to the edge of the opening. Colwyn was the first back on his feet, followed by the agile Oswyn, with Torquil a step behind. Together they helped the frantic Bardolph, then all turned to peer into the narrow gap.

There was light below, and not far below, at that.

"Ergo! Titch!" Colwyn shouted downward.

Below, Ergo was already examining their prison. Titch had landed hard and was a little slower to rise. The light was dimmer than in the corridor above, but they could still see clearly.

"We're here," Ergo replied.

"All right?"

"Except for bruises and bumps." He glanced over at Titch. The boy nodded once as he gingerly felt of his backside. "I'd guess we're about ten feet below you." He examined the smooth, curving walls. "I can't find a handhold big enough for a gnat. We're in another tunnel. It's very narrow."

Torquil bent over the gap and yelled down. "You're sure there's no way to climb up?"

"Only for a bird," Ergo told him.

Titch moved to stand closer to his friend, staring upward.

"Throw us a rope," Ergo shouted.

Torquil turned and began rummaging through his rucksack. The coil he produced was thin.

Colwyn eyed it uneasily. "Doesn't look very strong."

"It'll hold them if they come up one at a time." Torquil sounded confident. "I know. I've had occasion to use it when plying my trade. A man should know his tools." He thought a moment, added, "My old trade, of course."

Colwyn turned his face away so that the bandit leader would not see his grin. "I guess even a rope can redeem itself. Hand me the line and brace it."

Torquil nodded, wrapped a section of the rope around his waist, and handed one end to Bardolph while Colwyn played out the other over the edge of the gap. The two thieves steadied themselves.

Ergo's eyes were on the rope, but Titch saw something out of the corner of an eye, shouted a warning. "Slayers!" He pointed up the narrow tunnel.

Colwyn tried to see below, bending over, but the twists and turns in the floor hid the approaching danger. Immediately he looped the rope around his waist, tightened it.

"I'm going down."

"Why risk all we've gained if—" Bardolph began, but Colwyn eyed him so coldly the man went silent.

"I'm going down," Colwyn repeated, "and now! Torquil, be ready to bring us up at the signal."

Torquil leaned backward, clenched his teeth. "Say the word and I'll have you out like a moonbeam."

"Right. Easy now." He stepped over the edge and started to let himself down.

He was suspended halfway between upper and lower passage when a deep rumbling sounded from all around and the gap began to close as quickly and unexpectedly as it had opened. Torquil didn't wait for orders, nor was there time to discuss the matter.

"Up! Pull him up!"

Despite the combined strength, Colwyn's ankles barely cleared the opening before it shut tight beneath them, forming a solid, unbroken floor beneath their feet once more.

Colwyn sat back, staring grimly at the crack that mocked them. Titch and Ergo were trapped somewhere below . . . with Slayers. He kicked at the surface in frustration. Not even Rell could have pried that mass apart.

A hand touched him and he stared up at Torquil. The thief's expression was set. "They chose. We all chose."

"But the boy . . ." Colwyn's fingers touched the glaive. But as had happened with Rell, Ynyr's words held him back. If he did not conserve the glaive's power to confront the Beast, all would be wasted.

"They've given what they could," Bardolph added. "Let's be off from here."

Colwyn hesitated, then nodded and climbed to his feet. But he left another part of his soul behind in that corridor.

Ergo had stared helplessly as the ceiling had slammed shut overhead. Now he backed down the corridor, his mind working frantically, his eyes on the two approaching Slayers. There was no telling where the corridor led, perhaps to a dead end, perhaps to the Beast's lair, perhaps nowhere. He leaned around the curving wall, ducked back as a Slayer spear lashed out at him.

It might have been the fear in the boy's face that galvanized him to action, or some hidden reserve of cunning and knowledge. Colwyn had suspected it lay hidden beneath that buffoonish exterior all the time, while Ynyr had doubted it. Whatever the inspiration, Ergo abruptly did what he did best.

He even did it right this time.

A thunderous roar shook the tunnel. The Slayers paused, uncertain, then fired again. But this was no waddling, awkward human flying at them. Instead they confronted a quarter ton of angry, fast-moving tiger.

Titch clung to the wall where the tiger had nudged him and watched with wide eyes. No one knew if the Slayers had emotions. If so, it's certain that two died that day full of surprise.

XIII

The peasant looked up from his berry-picking and frowned. The sky was not cloudy, but there was thunder in the air. He rose, leaned on his staff and stared up the long, grassy valley. Beyond the mountains, perhaps, there might be a thunderstorm brewing.

A shape appeared in the air before him. It was very large, but it was not a cloud. He found himself backing away from it instinctively. It grew darker and more solid as he tripped and fell backward.

The Black Fortress sat silent and massive between mountain ridges as the peasant ran madly to warn his village. Its exterior was smooth and unchanged, giving no hint of the turmoil occurring within.

Colwyn held up a restraining hand and his companions slowed behind him. The corridor opened unexpectedly into a large, smooth-walled chamber with a high ceiling arching overhead. In the center stood a hexagonal dome of strange design and faintly threatening construction. It made Colwyn think of the war helmets worn by the fighters of distant Ulrathay. But what was one to make of those dark ridges that gave it support and the internally lit, translucent panels that bulged outward? No human hand had fashioned this place, and no human soul ought to abide within it.

Yet one particularly precious soul was thus trapped. Colwyn could sense it with every fragment of his being. He couldn't take his eyes from the structure. He knew where they were.

"Quietly now," he told them. "We're close to the center."

"The center of what?" Bardolph wanted to know. "Of the Fortress?"

"Of everything," Colwyn assured him.

Following his lead, they filed out of the corridor and spread out to inspect the hexagon of those softly lit panels. Not a man of the three doubted that it was any less solid than the outer walls of the Fortress. And like those outer walls, there was no sign of an entrance.

When they'd completed the brief inspection, Colwyn declared his intentions. "From here I must go on alone."

Torquil tried to see through one of the vitreous panels, fought to imagine the source of the strange inner light. "Go on to where? There's no way in. And if this is what you hint it is, I wouldn't expect some overanxious Slayer to jump out and offer us one. They won't make that mistake again."

"There are no Slayers here," Colwyn murmured. "This is the place of something else. But there must be a way in." He began backing a few steps away from the hexagon, studying it intently and paying but slight attention to his friends' movements. Torquil and the others moved to stand well behind him.

"There's nothing for it," the bandit leader announced. "That place is as solid as—" He caught himself as he saw

Colwyn remove the strange, five-armed weapon from its
holding loop. Colwyn's eyes were slightly glazed and he
seemed to be concentrating on something beyond their range
of vision.

"Get behind him," Torquil suddenly ordered his men.

"Why? What's he going to do with that?"

"Get behind, Oswyn, and you too, Bardolph. And be
ready." His hand went to his war ax.

"Ready for what?" Oswyn drew his own weapon, watched
as Colwyn held the glaive out in front of his chest.

"I don't know," Torquil replied irritably, his concentration
on Colwyn, "but be ready for it."

Suddenly five blades appeared on the glaive, one at the
terminus of each golden arm. Colwyn brought it back, then
flung it hard toward the hexagon. It whizzed toward the
nearest section of wall . . . and struck.

A thunderous chiming rang through the chamber. Oswyn
put his hands to his ears while the others winced, wondering
how so small a device could generate so violent a reaction.

The blades had failed to scratch the hexagon's walls and
the glaive returned to Colwyn's waiting hand. Oblivious to
the astonishment on the faces of his companions, he threw it
a second time, striking the same spot as before with uncanny
accuracy. This time a huge chunk of wall was blasted away.
Again he threw the glaive, and again, ignoring the overlapping
echoes that had forced his friends to their knees.

"He doesn't act like he hears the noise!" Oswyn shouted.
"He doesn't act like he hears *anything*!"

"What?" Torquil asked. He had his hands over his own
ears, trying to shut out the deafening echoes.

"I SAID, I DON'T THINK HE CAN HEAR THE
SOUNDS!"

"I DON'T EITHER!" Torquil agreed.

Colwyn advanced toward the dome like a wraith through a

dream, methodically catching and throwing the glaive, hewing a passage through the wall. Sweat poured off his face, and his muscles quivered with the effort. Throw, catch, throw, catch, and throw again. The blades of the glaive became nicked and dulled but the weapon itself remained as solid as the day he'd stolen it from its fiery vault. Shattered fragments of dome flew everywhere, striking walls and floor and ceiling impartially and forcing his men to dodge quickly. The only place in the chamber free of flying debris was the section of floor occupied by the slowly advancing Colwyn.

Someone else heard that steady ringing, muted though it was inside the dome. Lyssa backed away from the intensifying noise. Such announcements of destruction could herald many things, but she doubted the Beast's imminent arrival was among them. He had already revealed his noiseless entryway to the sanctuary.

That implied the presence of another party that sought to fashion its own entrance. The mere thought filled her with more hope than she'd dare allow herself since the day of her abduction. She divided her attention between the section of wall where the approaching sounds rang loudest and the dark hollow that had earlier produced the Beast.

The ringing in the chamber subsided somewhat as Colwyn dug his way deeper into the dome. Torquil removed his hands from his ears. The noise was bearable.

He turned to the other two. "Colwyn works difficult magic and we stand around like hogs waiting for our butchers. The noise is bound to draw Slayers. Colwyn has enough to work without having to worry about such distractions. Let's scout around this object. Surely we can provide a warm welcome for any black-eyed curiosity seekers."

Oswyn swung his mace. "I hope some of them do come. We'll satisfy their curiosity, all right. I owe poor Ergo a dozen dead souls at least."

"Not if I get to them first," Bardolph said tersely, testing the edge of his own weapon.

"I'm sure there will be plenty of killing to satisfy all of you," Torquil said. "Come on."

They started off to their left, intending to complete another circumnavigation of the dome. Bardolph followed for a moment, then paused.

"We ought to split up here in case they try to take us from behind. We can meet on the far side."

Torquil nodded approvingly. "A good idea, if there were more than three of us. I don't want anyone going off by himself. But we can at least spread out a little."

Torquil took the center, Bardolph the outside, and Oswyn crept along the wall of the glowing dome. Bardolph felt his way cautiously along the chamber wall, walking parallel to his companions.

And then the wall wasn't there anymore to support him, and yet its ghost was. His hand sank through the wall. There was no time to catch his balance, only time enough to shout.

"Torquil!"

Then he was gone, the wall having swallowed him up as neatly as quicksand had taken poor Menno. Torquil and Oswyn arrived an instant too late to help. They pushed and probed the wall, testing, searching for an opening. It was as solid as the floor under their feet.

For another second. Then it had vanished and both men tumbled forward. Torquil had silently cursed Bardolph for his clumsiness. There was no reason for a good thief to be caught so badly off balance, even by a trick wall. But as he stumbled inward, he apologized mentally to his friend, for it was as if they fell downward instead of just sideways, as though the wall turned everything inside out.

They fell into a small room. Bardolph was just getting to his feet. Torquil immediately regained his balance and ran at the wall behind them, only to discover that it had become a real wall once more, solid as granite.

"I leaned against it and suddenly everything was upside down," Bardolph told them.

"I know. It did the same thing to us. Idiots!" He slapped at his forehead. "Now we've gone and left Colwyn's retreat unprotected, and he may not even realize we've left."

Turning a slow circle, he took stock of their prison, a ten-by twenty-foot rectangle with no visible openings. There wasn't even an air vent, yet the atmosphere was thick and warm, if a touch musty.

The walls bristled with metal stakes and he knew they hadn't been placed there for decoration. He'd seen similar rooms in use in some of the less enlightened kingdoms and knew well their function.

He cut at the wall they'd tumbled through with his sword, barely scratching the material. "Search! Check the other end. We've got to get back!" Oswyn and Bardolph rushed to inspect the opposite end of the cell.

So far their prison was silent and still. Torquil did not expect it to remain that way for long. Something was toying with them, perhaps enjoying their anxiety. Soon it would become tired, or bored, or indifferent.

He wondered how many minutes they had left.

XIV

Lyssa backed away from the imploding wall. Shards of glassy material flew past her and dust stung her face. She ignored them, her gaze locked on the trembling surface. A crack appeared, was quickly enlarged by another blow from behind. A third strike blew a ten-foot-tall gap in the barrier.

Then a figure stepped through, clutching a strange, battered weapon, and she was running forward even before he saw her.

"Lyssa!" Colwyn opened his arms to her.

"I knew you'd come," she sobbed. "I knew that if any man could find me here it would be you!"

"I'd have cut a trail through the center of Krull itself to reach you." He pulled away from her kiss. "You don't look injured."

"My body is unharmed. It was my mind that had begun to worry me. I do not think I could have kept up hope forever." She spared a bitter glance for her prison. "It doesn't take long for the absence of light to kill a flower."

A soft thump reached them from across the chamber and Lyssa turned quickly toward it. "He always signals his approach, though whether to frighten or warn me I do not know."

Colwyn took a new grip on the glaive. "I have penetrated his lair and battled past every obstacle he's thrown at me. I'm not frightened."

"Be cautious, then, if not fearful, husband-to-be. He is nothing to underestimate."

"I never underestimate death, love. He is a sickness that must be banished from Krull." He showed her the glaive. "I have brought the right medicine to treat with."

"Not in here, Colwyn. This is his sanctuary. He is too powerful here. He seems to draw strength and comfort from this place, though I know not how. You must fight him away from the center."

"You know him better than I. I accept your strategy, wife."

He flung the glaive toward the far side of the chamber, above the place where faint pulses of light could be seen in the distance. The weapon struck the arch above the entrance, shattering it. A second throw buried the doorway with rubble.

"That will not prevent him from following," she told him.

"I do not expect it to. I buy time to prepare." He offered his hand. "Come."

Lyssa accepted his hand and together they made their way out through the gap he'd blasted in the wall, Colwyn glancing backward to make certain nothing sprang on them from behind.

The chamber outside the dome was not the flower gardens decorating the rear courtyard of the White Castle, but to Lyssa it seemed a step closer to paradise. She stepped out onto the smooth floor, relieved to be free of the Beast's sanctuary, and turned to await her lover.

Intent on the newly carved passageway into the dome, she failed to notice the Slayer that had materialized behind her. Its attention was not directed toward her but was focused on the emerging figure just beyond. It raised a long, glowing spear.

At the last instant she sensed movement behind her, turned, and shouted a warning. "Colwyn!"

He ducked instinctively and flung the glaive. Lyssa spun away from the flying splinters as the glaive shattered the spear and continued on to bury itself between the Slayer's eyes. It hung embedded until the Slayer began to topple, then arced back to Colwyn's waiting hand.

Lyssa eyed the sparkling weapon with amazement. "That is no device of recent manufacture."

" 'Tis older than you can imagine. A very wise man led me to it. Some day I'll tell you all about him. A fine story with which to regale our children. Children who will grow up in a world free of the Beast and his minions."

"Our children, yes," she whispered. "A good thought to cling to." She saw that he was looking past her. A glance revealed nothing but empty corridor beyond. "What troubles you, husband?"

"I did not come alone. There were others who've aided me and I see no sign of them."

"Which way did you come?"

He gestured toward the near tunnel. "Down that passage in a near straight line from the outside wall."

"Then perhaps they've gone on ahead to make sure the way out is clear. I'll go and see, if you wish to search this room."

"And have the Slayers take you a second time and carry you off to another cell? No. Stay here and search with your eyes if you wish, but I'll not be separated from you again."

She nodded understandingly. "There may not be time to search for anything." From within the dome the sound of rubble being pushed aside could be heard. "He comes."

"As good a place as any." Colwyn examined ceiling and

walls. "He would likely catch us in that tunnel. Here I have more room to maneuver." In any fight he'd always relied on his speed and quickness. Now was not the time to be trapped like a termite in some narrow corridor.

Nor would he abandon this place without learning the fate of his companions. Lyssa must understand that. A glance at her expression told him that she did.

At least they were together again, and together they would leave this place, on the plane of the living or of the dead. His fingers tensed on the glaive as he waited for whatever might emerge from the crack in the dome's wall.

A grinding noise brought the anxious Torquil to his feet. A quick look showed what he most feared: the opposing spikes of their prison walls had begun to advance slowly toward each other. Their captor had set the game in motion once again.

All three men moved to the center of the room. Then Bardolph was scanning the floor frantically.

"What's wrong?" Oswyn asked him.

"My knife. My golden dagger. There it is!" Before Torquil or Oswyn could put out a hand to restrain their companion, he'd bolted toward the far corner of the room. The dagger had fallen from his belt. Now it lay just beneath the lowest of the protruding spikes.

"Bardolph!" Torquil yelled. "Let it go! Don't be a fool, man!"

Ignoring him, the thief threw himself prone on the floor and stretched out a hand toward the gleaming weapon. Torquil ran up behind him and grabbed at his feet but Bardolph kicked him away.

"Leave me be! Ah, I've got it!" His hand closed around the dagger and he started to worm backward.

But the spikes were tight about his body and not even Torquil's strength could free him.

"Torquil!"

The bandit chief would have preferred that his friend breathe his last with another name on his lips. Too late now. He looked away as the spikes continued slowly onward, until they were locked tight through the twitching form. Save for shouting Torquil's name, Bardolph died quietly.

The walls continued closing on the two survivors, their progress slow but inexorable.

"Fool," Torquil mumbled, not looking at the body in the corner. "I told him once that that royal pigsticker would be the death of him!"

"Some men fix on certain objects the way others fix on women," Oswyn observed quietly as he studied the ceiling. "It's a madness. I like gold as well as the next fellow, but I value my life higher. Bardolph always was a gambler."

Torquil resisted the obvious rejoinder. They had more pressing matters to deal with, all of them long and pointed.

The flashing lights were brighter now. Colwyn tensed as he examined them, his gaze locked on the gap he'd cut through the dome's wall.

When the Beast fell upon them, however, it was from a different place. The monster exploded through the hexagon with as much disregard for the damage thus done as for any harm it might do itself. The ball of green flame it flung at Colwyn looked familiar. It was the same color as the Slayers' spears.

Colwyn barely had enough time to deflect the ball-lightning with the glaive. Though blocked, the fireball had passed near enough to graze his right side. His nostrils brought him the odor of burnt leather and fur. Wincing, he backed away from the alien colossus. A second blast of energy followed close upon the first, singeing him again.

The relentless onslaught would already have overpowered any dozen well-armed warriors. Ynyr had prepared him to deal with strength but not fury.

Colwyn halted. No more retreats, he told himself angrily. He was in this place, at this moment, from exercising his own will. There was no point in blaming Ynyr, who had done the best by him he could. Ynyr could not help him defeat the Beast. This was his own destiny, the destiny he'd crossed half a world to confront.

Think! Your opponent is mortal. Huge and intimidating, powerful and alien, but mortal. Use your skill. Press him hard. Wound his confidence if not his body.

The next time one of the green fireballs came toward him he dodged under and forward, deflecting it over his head and following through with the motion to fling the glaive at the Beast. It shattered another fireball in midair, sending tendrils of green flame in all directions. The weapon continued onward to rip into the Beast's arm.

The monster emitted a bellowing moan and clutched at himself. Staggering, it launched a much larger globe of energy. Hanging in space between the two combatants, the glaive shattered the fireball almost as soon as it left the Beast's grasp. Eyes damp with the sweat of concentration, Colwyn moved his hand through air. The glaive responded by swooping in a wide arc around the Beast's head.

Trying to dodge, the monster lurched to one side, crashing into the hexagon. At the same time, Colwyn's arm dropped. So did the glaive, burying itself so deeply in the creature's chest that only two blades remained visible above the skin. The Beast staggered and fell against the sanctuary, his great weight caving in the standing wall as he toppled. He lay motionless amidst the rubble, the flashes from the great body sparse and barely visible.

Colwyn extended a commanding hand, but try as he might, the glaive refused to return to its master's grasp. Lyssa stepped hesitantly clear of the corridor wall that had shielded her.

"Is it dying?"

"I don't know. I don't know how any living thing could survive a blow like that from the glaive. But it won't return to me. I think it must be too deeply buried to pull free." Cautiously, he approached the huge, immobile body.

Whereupon a hand moved; a massive, taloned hand, rising to cover the still embedded glaive. Colwyn backed away as the monster rose. It stood before them as though the blades buried in its chest troubled it no more than the pile of debris it contemptuously shoved aside.

Another fireball flew toward Colwyn, the largest the Beast had yet conjured, a swirling green planetoid that blinded both Colwyn and Lyssa with its power.

Somehow they managed to avoid it, running wildly down the corridor. It exploded behind them, tearing away a huge chunk of ceiling. Debris rained down about them as they raced for the shelter of a side tunnel.

The faked death had failed to dispose of Colwyn. For the first time he thought he could sense something like anger emanating from the monster. It was on its feet again, coming after them, the flashes from its body bright enough to light the dim chamber like midday.

Behind them a voice reached out, full of strength and the promise of unnatural death. "She will be *my* queen now!" the voice promised.

"The glaive is lost," Colwyn told her, panting hard as they ran. They entered a different kind of chamber, full of sharp projections rising from the floor and descending from the ceiling and walls. Anxiously they ran through the unsettling cavern, frantically searching side passages for a hiding place. "I have no weapons against him." Another fireball raced after them, exploding contemptuously against the ceiling. He could feel the heat of it as fiery splinters rained down around them. He turned into a branching passage.

"Colwyn . . . Colwyn, there's no peace for us in flight!"

He slowed, gasping for breath. She leaned against him, holding him tightly to her, trying to regain her own wind. There were no telltale flashes in the dark passage behind them.

For a second he thought they'd gained a respite . . . until he turned to see the pulsating glow *ahead* of them. Hopeless. It was hopeless. The Beast was content now to toy with them, to prolong the game.

Lyssa was shaking him, trying to gain his attention. He stared dully at her. "I've failed, my love. I'm sorry."

"Don't talk like that. Think! Those last two fireballs did not touch us, did not harm you."

"He doesn't want to damage you, so he is careful."

"Not that careful. Colwyn, I watched the fight. He directs his energies as you directed the glaive. He should have struck you twice."

"He'll kill me soon enough."

She shook her head violently. "No! Remember the first fireballs you dodged before you began to fight with the glaive?"

"I was fast and fortunate."

"More than that. It has to be more than that! It wasn't the glaive. It was you. The glaive was only a tool, a lens that enabled you to focus your energies. Consider, husband, the requirements of the marriage ceremony. The ability to bring a torch to life."

"A trick, nothing more."

"A trick how many could duplicate? None!"

"Ynyr," Colwyn muttered, his mind working furiously. "He told me that the Beast needed to keep us apart. I didn't understand. He tried to explain to me but the explanations went away with his life. And it's not me." He was suddenly excited.

"Half-right, you are half-right, Lyssa! It's not me the Beast fears. It's *us*. It's what we might do together."

She shook her head, frowning, confused. "No . . . I have no power, Colwyn."

" 'I take fire from water' . . . another 'trick'? He fears us, Lyssa." He leaned away from the wall as a fireball exploded close by his head.

"That's why he had to take you away from me. He needs to keep us apart."

"He spoke of sharing power with me." Her eyes shone even in the dim light. "What power could he want to share with me? I didn't think—"

"There is more to our union than an alliance between kingdoms, Lyssa. Between man and woman. Much more. Everything has felt so right. Ynyr . . . he was trying to tell me why. Our marriage . . . it was ordained, I think. Before either of us were born."

"You mean the spirits . . . ?"

"No, nothing supernatural. As we were conceived, so was a definite plan. I wish I could talk to my father! He would have clues to give me, if not explanations. I can sense it now."

"As can I, Colwyn."

"But I don't know what to do," he said helplessly. The flashing lights that signified imminent death were very close.

She took his hands in hers, drew him near. "Look at me. Concentrate. Think that the glaive still exists for you to fight with it. Fight with it, Colwyn. Fight with what matters."

He lost himself in her penetrating, intense stare. As he did so he experienced a resurgence of that strange inner trembling he'd felt many days ago when they'd stood together in the bowels of the White Castle, repeating the ancient vows. Something surged within him. He felt all that was Lyssa flowing out toward him, merging, melding, growing strong and bright.

Much of it was love ... but there was more.

"It will not return to me except from the hand of the woman I choose as my wife," he found himself repeating.

Lyssa was replying but he hardly heard her: "I give it only to the man I choose as my husband." She held out a clenched fist, opened the fingers to reveal the fire dancing on her palm. It had lain dormant there and elsewhere ever since her abduction from the castle. Now it burned furiously in her hand.

"Take the fire from my hand. In so doing may it become at last one with your own."

Smiling, his expression distant and serene, he reached out and touched her hand. The flame shot up his arm like a live thing, a fragmented and intensely powerful manifestation of something deep within them both.

He turned to confront the Beast, his arm and being alive with energy. A fireball came straight for him and he waved at it. It split to flow harmlessly around them as a wave crashes around a rock jutting out into the sea. Lyssa at his side, Colwyn started forward.

Uncertain and suddenly afraid, the Beast retreated. As he did so he flung a gigantic wall of writhing green flame at the advancing humans, taking no care this time to spare Lyssa. Colwyn gave it the back of his hand, blasting the green wall aside and sending it curling back on itself to strike the Beast's side.

The monster turned to flee. Colwyn struck at its legs, bringing it crashing to the ground. There was light in his own eyes now, not red but starlight-brilliant. As the Beast went down, Colwyn lavished fire upon it. Smoke rose from the body. It did not burn like human flesh, but was consumed with great speed and fury. The corpse contorted violently as it vanished. A great scream of pain and rage echoed throughout the Fortress.

Then it was gone. There were no more flashing lights, no more peculiar moans or confident threats. No more Beast.

A hand touched Colwyn's cheek as he dazedly continued to pour cleansing flame on the spot where the Beast had fallen.

"Gentle, my love. The thing is done."

He blinked, looked over at her, then back to the severely scorched floor. He held up his own hand, staring at the fire that burned there. "I did it, but I still don't know how."

"We did it, Colwyn. As you said we should. Truly that was the secret the Beast sought to keep from us. From all men. It failed, and from this moment on its time on Krull is over."

Colwyn clenched his fist and watched as the flame slid slowly down his arm to vanish between his fingers. The sand runs out, Ynyr had observed, but now something greater had come back to mankind. Somewhere the old man must be watching them, and feeling very pleased with himself.

The spikes were close to touching his belly, and Torquil had made final peace with himself when he noticed that the walls had abruptly stopped advancing. Oswyn opened his eyes, dared to touch one of the protruding spikes. He and Torquil exchanged anxious glances.

A dull cracking sound filled the room and a hole appeared in the far wall. Through it they could see the hexagon of the Beast.

Oswyn pulled at his friend but Torquil hung back, staring openmouthed at the walls as they drew back to their original positions. The retreat was uneven, the movement of the walls occurring in fits and starts, as if a spring or some other mechanism had failed somewhere deep within the Fortress.

The bandit leader did not rush for the exit. Instead, he slowly walked over to kneel beside Bardolph's limp, punctured body. Reaching out and over he picked up the golden dagger. Then he placed it back between Bardolph's clutching fingers and closed them over the hilt.

"He was a good man. Gold was his only weakness." A chunk of ceiling came crashing down nearby. Oswyn waited next to the miraculous gap.

"Hurry! The walls may close in again."

Torquil stood, oddly calm. "I think not, my friend. But I have no love for this place. The sooner we are free of it, the better I'll like it." Another section of roof fell in. He stepped around it and followed Oswyn.

Dust and rock fell around the embracing Lyssa and Colwyn as well. The corridor was alive with the sounds of disintegration. Something more than cement and nails had kept the Fortress intact. Now it was gone and the walls were coming down.

"The Fortress dies with its master. We must find Torquil and the others. My friends." He smiled at her. "You understand: I can't abandon them."

"I would not have a man as my husband who could do so." She kissed him gently and led him back the way they'd come when they'd fled from the Beast.

They did not have to search long. Torquil nearly bowled Colwyn over as the two men reached the corridor intersection simultaneously. He looked past the bandit chief, saw Oswyn and no others.

"Bardolph?"

Torquil shook his head. "Glory would have made him uncomfortable anyway. He preferred his gold." He nodded at the rumbling walls. "A fitting tomb for a man who never lived in anything grander than a thatched hut. We heard the sounds of battle, even through the walls that held us.''

"The Beast is no more.''

Torquil indicated the princess. "So I gathered by our sudden freedom, and the beauty that walks beside you confirms it.''

"I have learned what Ynyr did not have the time to tell me. We are free to leave.''

"We won't be if we stand here talking about how successful we've been,'' Oswyn reminded them. He moved past Colwyn and started up the corridor.

They followed, Colwyn and Lyssa running hand in hand, Torquil guarding the rear lest any remaining Slayers think to try and revenge their master.

Oswyn skidded to a halt, retraced his last couple of steps and pointed at the floor. "What do you make of this?''

Colwyn bent to stare at the bloody tracks that marred the otherwise smooth surface. Cat tracks, and a large cat by the look of it. He looked anxiously down the corridor.

"That's Ergo. It's got to be.''

"That tunnel doesn't lead outward,'' Torquil pointed out. "Maybe his sense of direction's failed him.''

"Maybe. They might also still be alive. Clearly he's hurt, and maybe the boy as well. Slayers might be keeping them from fleeing back this way. Stay here and guard the princess, my friend.'' Torquil nodded.

Colwyn turned to Lyssa. "These two risked their lives to help us. I can't leave here if there's a chance they're still alive.'' She nodded, watching anxiously as Colwyn and Oswyn raced down the narrow passageway, their eyes intent on the bloody tracks marking the floor. Dust and debris rained down on her and deep-throated rumblings sounded all around. They would have to hurry.

The two men rounded several turns before they came upon

Ergo, lying limply, his head resting in Titch's lap. Oswyn bent over him, checking his wounds.

"Cuts and bruises, but nothing fatal."

"There's a chance, then." Together they lifted the dazed Ergo to his feet, each man slipping beneath an arm, and half walked, half carried him back the way they'd come. The tunnel began to collapse behind them.

The Fortress was coming down around them, and it seemed that the rate of collapse was accelerating as they ran. Ahead lay the bridge they'd crossed on entering. No Slayers stood athwart it to block their retreat, but the unsteady span made the dark abyss below seem even deeper. They'd barely dashed across when the center of the arch cracked away behind them, to tumble into the bottomless depths beneath.

They turned a well-remembered curve and came to a halt. Ahead lay debris and huge blocks of solid material.

"This is where we entered," Torquil growled in frustration, "but the old entrance is gone, blocked." He flinched as a small piece of rock struck his shoulder. The Fortress was shaking like a pile of twigs. At any moment the last of the roof might come down atop them.

Colwyn shifted his half of the burden of Ergo, and Titch tried to help compensate. "Torquil, Oswyn, stand behind us. We'll make our own exit."

The two thieves obediently moved aside. Their eyes widened at what happened next. Oswyn muttered silent oaths, but Torquil expanded like a proud uncle. One more time, his decision to throw in his lot with this man was vindicated.

The tongue of flame Colwyn threw at the wall licked at the dark resinous substance and smashed through to the outside, reaching brilliantly into clear sky.

Then the way was clear, as the last of the fire vanished into the heavens, and they were clambering down the quivering flank of the Fortress. Colwyn was positive he'd never again feel anything as comforting beneath his feet as the grassy loam that greeted them at the base of the structure. He caught Lyssa as she made the last jump, swung her effortlessly to the ground.

Within the Fortress, the rumbling became a maelstrom of destruction.

"Is the whole thing going to collapse?" Oswyn asked as they moved away across the field.

"I don't know, but we're still too close. Hurry yourself!"

They increased their pace until they'd run a respectable distance across the field. There the exhausted Oswyn chose a thick patch of grass and flowers and gently lowered Ergo to the ground. Lyssa joined him in tending to the smaller man's injuries.

Torquil shaded his eyes as he and Colwyn stood side by side, studying their former prison.

"It's falling to pieces, all right," Torquil observed. "And something else."

Colwyn said nothing, merely nodded and watched. Torquil's comment was premature. As they looked on, the massive structure abruptly fell in on itself with a great roar, almost as if in the final measure the monolith's internal support was little more than fury and nightmares.

Then the earth shook beneath their feet as the pile of rubble slowly rose into the air. It moved languorously at first but rapidly picked up speed, rising heavenward until it was lost to sight.

Somewhere a bird let out a hesitant cheep. Insects resumed their buzzing and small furry things peeked out of tiny holes. The grass that had been crushed flat beneath the Fortress's immense bulk began to straighten, responding to the return of light and air. In a few days none would be able to tell what had so recently afflicted the peaceful valley.

"Let's hope we never see its like again," Colwyn murmured.

"The Beast was its power and you destroyed the Beast,"
Torquil pointed out. "It's gone forever."

Both men turned around as a sharp cough sounded.

"Ergo!" Titch shouted delightedly as the injured man
opened his eyes.

"He'll be all right," Lyssa told the boy.

Ergo let his gaze focus on the woman seated nearby. "I
must be in paradise," he mumbled. He saw the others
standing nearby, eyeing him solicitously. "You are the princess? The one we sought to free from the Beast?"

She smiled. "Yes."

"He was right. You are worth dying for." He let his head
lie back on the cushioning grass. "And there is blue sky
overhead, and clouds, and I smell wild pepper and other
growing things. We've won."

"Yes," she told him, "you've won."

Titch leaned close. "I owe you my life, magnificence."

"Think nothing of it," Ergo replied, his spirits rapidly
returning. "As you know, I specialize in trifles." Titch couldn't
repress a grin.

"Ah, boy, I should have stuck to puppies."

"Oh no," Titch said, speaking to the others. "You should
have seen him! He turned himself into a giant of a tiger and
took on a whole army of Slayers." His words were filled with
admiration and amazement.

"He cut them all down, all by himself."

"Go on, boy," Ergo urged him. "Now tell them how I
nearly bested the Beast myself, though I fought with one
broken leg and my left arm numb at my side." Titch tried to
respond, but dissolved in boyish laughter, unable to lie and
giggle simultaneously.

"We'll have to see about getting you that puppy, boy. One that doesn't disappear every time you doze off."

"Really? You think so?"

Ergo nodded. "I am quite positive."

Colwyn smiled at the exchange, suddenly remembered something almost forgotten. He reached for the chain still hanging about his neck, removed the gold key hanging from it and handed it out to Torquil.

"I think it's time now you unlocked those manacles, don't you agree?"

Torquil hesitated, studying the metal bands encircling his wrists. "You know, I think I'd like to keep them, as a memento of our little journey. Have them gilded someday, if I can afford it." He moved to hand the key back to Colwyn, who refused it.

"No, the key is yours."

Torquil scratched at his beard. "Only the king and his lord marshal have the right to carry this key."

Colwyn's grin widened. "That's right," he said briskly, and turned away to resume his conversation with Lyssa. Torquil frowned in confusion, eyed the key. As realization took him, his frown turned to a grin, then a wide smile. He chuckled, then roared with delight at the irony of it all.

His laughter echoed across the open field, bounced gently off grass and flowers as the little troupe started northward through the valley.

Northward, toward home.